# TRAVEL NOTES

(FROM HERE—TO THERE)

✧

STANLEY CRAWFORD

# Travel Notes
(from here—to there)

© 1967, 2014 Stanley Crawford

first Calamari Press version, 2014
ISBN: 978-1-940853-02-4

originally published by Simon & Schuster, 1967

designed by Cal A. Mari using original cover by Lawrence Ratzkin
& back cover photo (of Stanley Crawford) by R. Wilton

published by Calamari Press, NY, NY

< www.calamaripress.com >

To C.H. and R.J

'All landscape is moral'

I. SO TO SPEAK

⁃

The airport was a shack. People sitting on boxes and luggage for lack of space to stand in, and the room or rooms were filled with smoke, with whispering, while a man perhaps the pilot pushed back and forth, climbing over legs and cartons with a sheaf of pink papers in his hand. His cap was thrust back on his head and a cigarette, in spite of a long holder, dribbled ashes down his coat. They were dressed in black, the people waiting, bundled up against the cold which blew in through the cracks of a window covered with newspaper, and it was almost dark outside from the low black clouds.

We were in there for over an hour. I had to hold a child on my knee.

They rolled back a heavy door and the wind blew in and the people in black stood up and pressed back so the boxes and luggage could be cleared away, and we went out. Everyone was quiet; it was hard to talk in the cold wind. An icy blast. Across a long red heated carpet to the plane which, I learned later, they had spent all that time waxing. It did indeed sparkle despite the gloom, and the ten waxers stood at attention as we climbed aboard. There were not enough seats to go around: half the passengers sat on their luggage in the aisle, while the rest of us, who were not much better off, held ours in our laps. Next to me was a young lady with a fortunately barkless dog, and she told me right off (in response to a question) that she was going there just to take some pictures. That was the extent of our conversation; the plane was too crowded for more.

The hostess was blind.

From the window I could see them starting the engine on my side, now hear the other one follow. A rough noise, such as one expects. The waxers in white overalls pulled blocks from under the wheels and went to the nose of the plane, to which they attached a chain, and pulled, or so I assumed from fragments of gestures I saw, and it did seem reasonable. Now we were rolling, faster and faster, and finally we passed them. They waved.

Because of the war and subsequent neglect the runway was in bad condition—pocked, grass sprouting from cracks, wavy stretches, potholes, piles of paper, old lumber, rotting tires, stray chickens—but our pilot, by judiciously raising whichever landing gear was threatened by an obstacle, made the run in the standard time of seven hours, forty-five minutes without incident. I slept most of the time, there being little to see beyond the interminable concrete which sloped gently down to sea.

My young lady traveling partner, who reminded me of my wife, left the plane with a curt remark to the effect that she knew this thing would never get off the ground.

Later I was to see her taking a picture of the moon. She could have done that anywhere.

✦

The car waiting at the airport took me all the way to the hotel, where I'm staying now. It is the most modern in this sizable city in the shadow of a purple range of mountains. The shower and toilet work fine, though one must enter the hall to reach them from my large and comfortable room, which is on the top floor with a view of everything there is to be seen. The desk or table, which appears to be of something like walnut, is suitable for writing, and did I carry valuables I would store them in its strong drawer, which has a lock and key. The bed, hard and narrow, is as my preference, and the four walls are patterned in a network of blue and violet flowers which form a nice bluish haze in the light of late afternoons, but in the bright of noon are quite maddening.

My only complaint is with the service. As I was lying in bed this morning, checking out the tape recorder I have brought along to record songs and what have you, the room-service girl walked in with a tray and said (the recorder was on):

'Good morning. This is your breakfast.'

'Your blouse—' which is my voice just as I cut off the machine.

The material of her blouse was of a pattern identical to the wallpaper, clearly the commercial motif of the establishment, and as a result I had, for an instant, the distinctly piercing impression that she was emerging from the very wall, not the doorway. So I have inadvertently recorded that brief dialogue, the young woman's thick accent, the rattle of dishes on a tray, the opening of the door, the three taps of her knock; and perhaps I should have left the machine on, but there would have been little else on the tape: she withdrew quickly, buttoning her blouse on the run.

My complaint is: not only was her blouse unfastened at the top, but for lack of a brassiere her breasts, shapely as they might have been, were almost completely exposed.

The desk clerk advised me that I should not miss the Famôus Lake, which I have never heard of and told him so. He insisted that it was known throughout the world and showed me a brochure to prove it. A small black-and-white photograph of a lake above the caption, The Famôus Lake, written in nineteen languages. Well, I will go see it. A car with a driver and interpreter is due here some time this morning. I will not be coming back here at any rate.

I must pack my suitcase in a moment.

✦

It is hard to describe the desolation of the first part of our trip. Flat but rough countryside with the purple mountains in the eastern distance, and at their feet clumps of trees—either forests or orchards—although the portion of the plain traversed by the road was without vegetation beyond brush and dry grass upon which grazed herds of a long-horned sheep or goat or cow, the interpreter being none too clear on just what they were. The narrow dirt road went up and down, over crests and into gullies, across a terrain which seemed flat from a distance but close up proved to be eroded and rumpled.

The car was a new model and I sat in the back seat, occasionally attempted to engage the interpreter in conversation. He spent most of the time arguing with the driver. I assumed the subject was political. These are a race of sandy-haired (almost golden), green-eyed men who all have a slightly dissipated air about them which suggests a potentiality for instantaneous vice. They speak with a slow twirling movement of the right hand, such as one will use in setting the hands of a large clock. At one point the interpreter stopped arguing long enough to turn around to ask me if I was married, and if married where my wife was.

'Traveling,' I said. I took advantage of this break to ask him about the Famôus Lake. Neither he nor the driver, he said, had ever been there but knew people who had. Probably very few, for when the car broke down three hours out of the city we had not met or passed a single other vehicle on the dirt road.

It was on a level stretch just beyond a narrow-gauge railway crossing. We got out and the driver lifted the hood, now addressed a long, earnest speech at me, which the interpreter simplified by telling me the driver was explaining that he would have to take it apart. I said he could do what he wanted, it was his car. The interpreter pulled me aside and told me how much the driver wanted for fixing it, and I slipped him the amount, which he stuffed into the driver's pocket.

With that, I wandered off to inspect the immediate countryside. Boulders, cacti, lizards, small moth-like creatures, and growing in the north shadows of rocks a little blue flower whose fragrance I cannot describe. The railway lines seemed all but abandoned. The rails were rusty, with one even missing, and many of the ties had been reduced to a yellowish powder by hordes of termites. Some distance from where the road crossed the tracks, there was a small structure, a sort of hut or shed open on one side and containing a bench beneath a timetable which, if I understood correctly, indicated that there were trains going to the Famôus Lake every seven minutes. Or would be. Or something was happening every seven minutes. The timetable was engraved on the finest of paper, and under the lower margin, rich in flowery motifs, was the inscription: The American Bank Note Company.

After seven minutes, nothing happened. I went back to the car.

I had probably given the driver too much money. The proper technique, I have been told but always forget, is to give them half of what they ask for. He and the interpreter had their coats off and shirtsleeves rolled up, the front of the car was scattered around in pieces and they were now hoisting the motor out with a block and tackle. I sat down on a rock and watched from a distance. Every now and then the interpreter would stand aside and read a page from the repair manual and translate it to the driver, and then they would go back to work. Soon they had the motor out of the car and positioned on a newspaper spread out in the middle of the road. As far as I was concerned, it was time for lunch. Yet they went on, unbolted the engine, laid the nuts and bolts and various parts in neat rows across the road until the motor was entirely disassembled. Now seemed a better time to interrupt them.

I told the interpreter I was getting hungry. At my words the driver stared at the interpreter anxiously, but upon hearing a translation resumed his normal bland but slightly menacing expression.

Then I heard the sound of an express train hurtling by, close by, fifty feet away, but I saw nothing, nothing at all. It may have been a gust of wind.

It was decided that we should go forage for food. The driver took a .22 revolver from the glove compartment and we set off down a narrow ravine a few hundred yards long and which opened into a small grassy meadow where grazed a herd of longhorn hairy cows (it might have been your yak, come to think of it, but with udders?) and we walked among them. The driver inspected the smaller, younger ones and reached some sort of agreement with the interpreter and shot one dead. At the sound of the gun, the other beasts retired to a corner of the meadow and lowed in unison at the perfectly blue sky.

Now we had to carry the carcass back to the road. The long horns and hair were suited to this purpose, but the ravine, being narrow and rocky, was no fit path of return, so instead we dragged the beast up a long but gentle slope to one side of the meadow, at the top of which we found a splendid panoramic view to rest at. From here you could see the railroad tracks looping down to another part of the plain, and not far below us (we had actually been closer in the meadow, but the view was blocked) sat a puffing steam engine and a dozen brightly painted passenger cars. It was a fine day, and many people were leaning out of windows or sitting on steps or in chairs placed here and there on the well-kept lawns and truck gardens which bordered the tracks, and children played around the women who were washing clothes in tubs next to the engine from whence issued, I imagine, a liberal supply of hot water.

I asked the interpreter what the name of this village was, and he replied that it was untranslatable, that it would come out only in numbers. Noticing my interest, the driver made a gesture of disgust, and we continued on our way.

By the time we dragged the animal back to the car I was starving and dead-tired and wanting to know why we had not brought the cow—they seemed quite docile—back under its own power. But there are questions you do not ask: if you start, everything becomes an argument. The bottom falls out. I am traveling to see, not to dispute. That is why I carry no camera. Suffice to say that my great hunger was satisfied when the driver piled brush in the road beyond the disassembled motor and roasted the hindquarters. I never tasted meat so tender. It was like chicken, or soft fish. I ate at least a pound of it, garnished with a salad made of those indescribably fragrant blue flowers I saw earlier, tossed in a hubcap by the interpreter.

We were no more than finished, and I in the mood for a nap, when a bus arriving from the opposite direction drew to a dusty halt at our bonfire. I expected we would have to clear everything out of the road—the motor parts, the rest of the car, the embers—but that wasn't the case. It is never the case. Nonetheless I withdrew to the side of the road and sat down on the ground with a boulder as a backrest. The bus driver and some twenty passengers, mostly soldiers, got out and conferred with my driver and interpreter, and after a while they threw the rest of the cow on the fire and settled down to a good hearty lunch.

I slept.

※

Their lunch was more protracted than ours and when I awoke they were still eating, and the sun was nearing its inevitable plunge into the very distant sea and soon the sky lay upon the darker horizon of water like a wall, pale under indirect lighting, and impenetrable. I shall pass over that night briefly. Our very late dinner consisted of an even larger cow slaughtered by the soldiers in the meadow and carried back to a bonfire so hot it singed the front of the bus. After dinner there took place what I can only describe as a community hum, but of tones much too low to be successfully recorded on my expensive machine. (It came out as a long buzz punctuated by whistles, applause and popping sparks from the fire.) The bus was loaded with casks of a local liqueur; this was consumed in liberal quantities. I had a swallow. What it resembles, I am not sure, though I have tasted something like it before. I failed to mention there was a woman in the crowd. When everyone but myself was drunk she offered herself to all takers, that is, one by one clockwise around the fire, and withdrew with her partners to the back of the bus. At my turn the interpreter gave me a quizzical look across the flames, then came round and said he didn't know the word to use.

'Copulate?' I asked.

Now he recognized it and asked me whether I wanted to. I declined. He turned and addressed a long and earnest speech to the assembled travelers, who listened intently and cheered and applauded, especially at the end. I thought it an excellent opportunity to excuse myself and go off to sleep in the back of the car, and indeed no one stopped me. But I met a restless sleep, for a full moon was up and the shades over the windows would not close tightly, and the reveling around the bonfire kept on beyond midnight, and now when all was finally quiet I was pulled from sleep by a distant crash, caused, as I learned the next morning, by a speeding victoria or similar carriage colliding with the back of the bus: the horse was killed on the spot. Nor was that all. I regret to say. Sleep is a precious commodity, not to be undervalued. Shortly before dawn I was aroused by a gnawing sound just outside the window I was resting my head against; it went on and on with a drowsy monotony while I wondered whether to move an arm, a head, to unroll the window and look out—suddenly there was an explosion, a hissing noise—and the car sank down a few inches. I was momentarily petrified. And now outside there was a scampering of feet and a long baleful cry which became more and more distant, and I wondered whether to have the tire changed now or later, and perhaps then I slept.

Just at dawn my driver and interpreter staggered in the front doors and fell into a long, noisy sleep.

When the sun came up over the purple mountains I was driven by foul odors inside the car to seek fresher air outside. There was no one else up yet except the young lady of the bus, and she was facing its side, combing her hair in the reflection of the metal. Only now did I recognize her as the woman who had sat next to me on the plane. We nodded. These are dark-haired (indeed, the hair is black), blue-eyed women who seem to be almost of a different race from the men who are theirs. The night air had laid a fine coat of dew over everything, and under the low warm sun rusting engine parts flamed in an indescribable manner. At the back of the bus, the dead horse lay spread-eagled on the ground beneath the carriage. From there too came sounds of snoring. It was a memorable scene.

Yet I had to suffer the most terrible boredom until noon when everyone awoke, when everyone slowly emerged from the vehicles, yawning, slapping their heads.

After breakfast (the horse, roasted behind the bus) it was decided to dismantle the bus and carry it piece by piece around the obstruction created by our car and to reassemble it on the other side. This procedure would have been perfectly sensible—given the way things were—had it not been for the fact that the reassembly area overlapped the railroad tracks which, I probably neglected to say, had an ominous air about them. Every seven weeks. I said good morning to my interpreter and driver in the hope of stumbling upon a tactful way to broach my doubts, but on mingling with the crowd I sensed high spirits, good humor and unanimous enthusiasm—and that was all I said. Not one word more.

What I am trying to describe took three or four days in all. I became grubbier and grubbier, acquired something of a beard, suffered from constipation, and whiled away the hours keeping my white linen suit clean.

I must speak now of my one attempt to do something more ambitious, and its failure.

In the course of my travels I anticipate many untracked or impenetrable regions where the knowledge of the use of firearms will mean the difference between life and death, so I borrowed the taxi driver's .22 pistol. A very fine weapon it was, and the rough plain seemed ideal for target practicing. After creating a safe distance between myself and the others, I stopped some fifty feet before a large boulder on the top of which a shepherd or cowherd had placed a neat row of stones. I raised and fired six times in rapid succession, scoring no hits.

I knew I should do better than that. Pistol reloaded, I raised my arm and fired—but in that briefest of instants between the will and the squeeze, or between the squeeze and the bang, a head emerged from behind the boulder, now vanished—an apparition so fleeting I could not be certain whether I had hit it.

I approached the boulder. My footsteps crunched in the sand. I peered over the rough top of the rock and there, on the other side, reclining on a mat or pile of soft vegetation, was the woman of the bus. Seeing I meant no harm, she stood up, quite nude except for one of those fragrant blue flowers thrust into her hair at the temple. Or some sort of plastic flower. I asked her how she was. She said she was fine. Perhaps, I suggested, she might like some kind of refreshing drink, as lying in the sun like that was quite enough to make you very thirsty. She thanked me but said no, she was not really thirsty yet. I asked her how she liked traveling. She said she found it very rewarding. Indeed. So it appeared. Well!

But it was clear she was waiting to resume sunbathing, so I withdrew, silencing the many questions that rose in my mind, the answers to which I may never know. And thanked my lucky stars she was not my wife, who would have made a scene, unutterable and interminable; she too travels, but never do we cross paths. Never.

I returned to my stone by the side of the road. Whole days passed. Just like that.

The bus was stripped piece by piece and carried to the other side of our car, the parts laid out in neat rows the length of the road over a distance of a hundred and fifty feet or more. The people of the carriage took over the business of tending the fire and slaughtering, while the young lady arranged continuous entertainments, from noons on, in the little shed by the railroad tracks. I later learned she was called the Païnted Wōman.

One of these days, around noon, when the last piece of the bus was being lifted over our car by chanting soldiers, I heard in the distance a sound like music and scanned the horizon to see where it was coming from. It could not be said that I was not expecting it: for there, a mile or so down the railroad tracks, was a bright glittering which seemed to be advancing towards us. I ran into the crowd and found my interpreter, who was carrying a basket of bolts, and pointed down the tracks.

'"Where" does that "train" "go"?' I asked.

He shielded his eyes against the sun. Or against my intense look. Now he told me it was the Famôus Lake Express bound indeed for the Famôus Lake. I suggested that it might be better if I caught the train since (I kept this to myself) the proceedings here had an interminable air about them. Even did I hint that I might invest in tickets for himself and the driver.

He repeated my question in several languages, each with a loud laugh. Some of the soldiers overheard, and soon we were surrounded by all, the center of a heated discussion. I stood and smiled. When one understands nothing it is best to feign the idiot, both easy and foolproof. Much pushing and shoving radiated inward from the outer ranks of the circle. My interpreter waved his hands, shouted everyone into silence with a verbal torrent, now went on towards a softly worded conclusion. That is, there seemed to be words in here, though when you listen to a foreign language you can never be certain. And when the gathering broke up, he turned to me and explained something to the effect that his country was thus.

I quite agreed. But instead of resuming work everyone stood at the side of the road to watch the glittering approach down the railroad tracks, which were blocked at the road by a heap of side panels and windows from the bus. The wind-blown strains of music, previously neither this nor that, were becoming distinguishable, and on the odd chance that something might come through I switched on my tape recorder: a marching tune, a cheerful piece I have heard many times before but don't know the title of. Now the glittering neared, cleared and went distinct as of many shiny horns, trumpets, trombones, tubas, drums and tambourines, as played by some fifteen men dressed in colorful blue uniforms and white-plumed golden helmets and riding a long bicycle-like conveyance of a certain grace and bounciness; it was trailed by a second bicycle car, pedalled vigorously in unison by another dozen men, to which was linked a third car, all tubular and spindly but entirely empty; and as the train neared in all elegance, thin spokes flashing in the sun, banners flapping, the young woman emerged from her shed to wave. The band played on, past her, towards the blocked crossing, and now nearly there, the instruments began to fade one by one and the band members and pedalers turned at us and stared.

Suddenly there was a rush. I gasped. The soldiers burst forth with a cry and leaped over boulders and crashed through brush and ran at the train. My driver and interpreter hastily joined them. I saw panic and utter confusion: the band and pedalers scrambled from the still-moving train and ran off in terror before the onrush of soldiers, some of whom set off in pursuit while others fell upon the cars, pushed them from the tracks and stamped, smashed, stomped and tore them all to bits.

Soon the other soldiers gave up pursuing the train people, who could be seen running on the horizon, leaping over rocks, blowing their horns and beating their drums, sounds which presently faded into nothingness.

Such was the end of the Famôus Lake Express. Upon catching his breath, my interpreter informed me of the amount the bus driver was demanding. I wanted to know exactly what for and so asked; he waved his hand around and indicated everything, or everybody, and as the amount was quite modest I paid it. From now on everyone worked with renewed energy.

✦

Or so I thought.

Upon regaining my by now habitual spot, a boulder by the side of the road where the bus had been, I noticed directly opposite, on the other side of the road some fifteen yards distant, a fellow sitting on the ground using another boulder as a backrest. He was staring across at me with a very special intensity. His face was vaguely familiar, as of my own. I couldn't recall seeing him before, but then the bus had been in the way. These days have been tiring. I dropped my head and took a nap.

When I woke up I realized that the bus was no closer to reconstruction; its parts still lay in the neat rows of many hours before, and no one at all was working on the car. Yet, to the other side of the railroad tracks, something was being done with great energy. I stood up, brushed off my suit and went over. The soldiers and various bus passengers had been divided into two groups: those carrying large stones from all over the plain to put in a pile, and those digging some trenches. My interpreter was crouched over a series of lines scratched in the sand. I bent over and looked carefully. Very nice, I said, very nice indeed.

Yes, replied my interpreter absently, he thought it would do. This, he added, pointing with a twig in his hand, this would be the living room wing, that the first bedroom wing, with two bedrooms and a bath at the end of the hall, and here the large dining room with a picture window viewing the purple mountain range, there the second bedroom wing, similar to the first, and the adjoining kitchen. The garage would be over there, he pointed in a vaguely westerly direction. Somewhere. Very nice, I said, watching the soldiers digging out the foundations, but who was it going to be for? My interpreter yawned and said the Païnted Wōman.

So I left him to his plans and walked back down the road, across the tracks. I could see now that things were definitely becoming interminable. There would be several months work in that building, perhaps even a year. And there I drew the line: I would not pay for it. Thus, mentally, I fired my interpreter, driver— the whole lot. They were not interested in going anywhere. The truth, at last, was out.

Yet, none of this would help me move on, I reflected while standing beside my habitual boulder, not at all. I wondered about the fellow sitting across the road, whether he was in a similar situation. But no sooner did I glance than he was on his feet and advancing towards me. His gait, already of a peculiar oiliness, was enhanced by the strangeness of his costume, a pair of overalls whose seams were sewn with what turned out to be tiny blue sequins which flashed continuously in the sunlight, along with countless golden charms fastened in random patterns everywhere except for—as I was to discover later—the seat of the pants; on his head was a sort of peaked leather cap, a pair of colored goggles dangled from his right hand.

He stood right before me now, looking me over. And I the same. Finally he introduced himself as the part-time aviator. How was I? Fine, and a professional traveler. He smiled. Yes, but things were now in a bad way, I said, explaining what was going on over there and that I was about to set off on foot for the Famôus Lake since there seemed to be no other way. Excusing myself for seeming to criticize his country's transportation situation, which was becoming deplorable. He replied no, he was not from here at all, just passing through. Still, his accent in English was quite thick, he had the same sandy hair and green eyes as the natives, but I would not argue. Perhaps he had good reason for not telling the truth.

We paced up and down the dirt road for a time in silence, until he said, in the most confidential tones, that as the part-time aviator he had, of course, an airplane. You don't say. Yes, a very fine vintage amphibious biplane. And where, I asked, was it now? He replied, did I see the dismantled bus, then did I see the liqueur casks that had been on the top rack, then to one side but partly concealed by them, did I see a sort of grey shroud? Yes. Under that, wings folded up, was his biplane. And if we could somehow manage to get the machine away from the others, he would most gladly drop me at the Famôus Lake before going on his own way. I saw, of course, what had happened to the Famôus Lake Express.

Exactly, I replied. So we hit upon a plan to escape.

Night fell again with a sunset of clangorous color, and the people of the bus and taxi gradually assembled in the foundation rectangle of what would be a spacious living room, before an already half-built stone fireplace of no mean dimensions. Here another cow was put to roast. The part-time aviator and I ate with them, then stole away separately in the darkness as soon as the local liqueur began to produce its traditional effect, and met up again at the shroud. Fortunately there was almost a hundred yards of night separating us from the building foundations, and we were able to roll the biplane through the bus pieces undisturbed, past the dismantled taxi, where I picked up my suitcase, and down the open road.

The part-time aviator considered it wise to proceed thus a

mile or two, hopefully out of sight, before stopping to spend the night. Then we would fly off at the crack of dawn. Unless they missed us tonight, they would probably not be awake until we were safely in the air. The road being flat and the biplane light of construction, pushing was an exercise both mild and refreshing. The moon soon rose, perfectly illuminating the road across the plain, the mountains and the distant sea. To pass the time of our pushing walk, I asked him what he did when he wasn't flying, since he was an aviator. He replied with a sigh that the question was a difficult one to answer, for it led one into the labyrinthine banality of accounting for minutes and years, which after all were long over and done with, of accounting for cities and chairs long-since forgotten, as unused, as given over to others. Who sprang up everywhere, ravenously wrenching away time and place, or what you had been deluded into thinking was yours. His purchase of the vintage amphibious biplane had taken care of that. Naturally it could not be used all the time. So, as I could easily see, when he wasn't flying he was doing simple things like walking along a road at night, things like eating, sleeping, things like explaining to people like me what he did when he wasn't flying.

After an hour's pushing, we reached a sort of depression in the plain where we could not be seen from the distance whence we had come, and here decided to spend the night. The part-time aviator pulled the shroud off the biplane and laid it down on the ground for himself, then retrieved a sort of blanket from the luggage compartment for me. I spread this out on the other side of the biplane, immediately dropping into a very sound sleep.

✢

At the crack of dawn I rose refreshed and doubly happy to be on the open road again. The sliver of sun inching over the distant purple mountain range shone with a special brilliance, and in this new light I examined the vintage biplane which I had not seen well the night before. A handsome thing if ever there was one, what with its black leather fuselage fitted with two open cockpits, its wings of gold, shiny as if dipped in gilt, but as yet unfolded, its attractive propeller, and so on. Little doubt in my mind: an airplane. Ambling around to the other side of it, there I found the part-time aviator's overalls stretched on a sort of wire rack, bent in the form of a man, where they must have been put in the dark of the night, and the part-time aviator himself, sitting on the ground some way off, clutching the shroud around him like a tent. We matched intense stares and said good morning. He sniffed the air a moment, then jumped to his feet, letting the shroud fall away, and proclaimed that today would be a perfect day to fly in the nude. What? I was sorry, I didn't hear correctly. Or see. For an incredible illusion was staring me in the face. I turned and examined the overalls still on the rack, now looked back at him. He was in fact quite naked, but of body totally tattooed in a manner so realistic, so resembling the forms and patterns of the distant overalls, that there was virtually no distinguishing the one from the other. Providing, I imagine, that one had seen the overalls first, as I had. Otherwise I do not know.

I bestowed him a brief compliment on the effect; he replied that he was especially proud of those parts of the tattoo which reflected, and I could not but express yet more amazement.

Now would I please stand back? Of course. A few feet more. Yes.

Clambering over the wings, which were folded back flat against the fuselage, he lowered himself into the first cockpit and assumed a pose, slightly bent forward, of the greatest concentration. I waited, half-expecting the propeller to spin to life. A long minute passed. Another. I sat down on a rock. Suddenly the air was rent by a great whacking noise, a blinding flash, and there stood the wings unfolded, quivering slightly, glinting in all their glory. The part-time aviator turned to me with a modest smile and climbed out of the cockpit.

The engine was now started in the conventional manner, that is, by giving the propeller a good yank. It spun around a few times with a whishing noise, until stopped by air drag. The part-time aviator repeated this gesture a number of times, to the same effect, and then said we should climb in the plane. So we made ourselves comfortable. I hesitated to point out that neither the engine was firing nor the propeller turning, except when stirred by an occasional gust of wind, and in the end I remained silent. For he was now talking excitedly, twisted around half-facing me, one hand on the stick, which he moved this way and that every now and then, and the ailerons squeaked, and on and on he went, recounting his adventures which, though patented, are all so far-fetched and unbelievable that I cannot begin to describe them.

I whiled away the time, the chatter, by examining the dirt road upon which we still sat, the almost barren plain, the distant mountains and sea, and other things, until with night and darkness the part-time aviator fell asleep and I was able to slip away from the biplane and, suitcase in hand, resume the way which was mine.

✧

The Famôus Lake Grand Hotel, built before the war, is a large and comfortable establishment and I have a room on the top floor. Except it has no toilet. (That is a long story which I cannot tell.) But the room is as I prefer it, quite simple, almost spartan: a bed where I lie, an angular walnut desk with spindly legs, or it might be more accurate to call it a sort of writing table, for there is but a solitary drawer fitted with a sturdy lock; a plain blue carpet on a hardwood floor, and walls papered in a pattern of tiny bouquets of violets alternating with an unidentifiable blue flower. This is curious: the violets are most realistically drawn while the little blue flowers are, to say the least, incredible. And to my immediate left a nightstand laden with current issues of local magazines, while out the door—and its very strong slide latch which I foolishly forgot to close—is a hallway decorated with old prints and photographs. And so on. I was planning to stay over here an extra day to rest up but am not sure whether I can (stand it), in spite of its permanently reduced rates.

The hotel occupies an attractive and isolated site overlooking the Famôus Lake. It is said to be the deepest lake in the world. In fact, either it is an ordinary large blue lake or something beyond description. If these travel notes are to be effective and useful I must make up my mind about such things, and fairly soon. The manager's living son relayed this proverb to me over breakfast: the people of the capital know the Famôus Lake better than the people of The Famôus Lake (the town about five miles across from the hotel)—which may not be clear to the armchair visitor, unless he understands that the lake went dry the year the hotel was built, drunk up (as water supply) by the thirsty citizens of the capital.

It has been almost impossible to work on my notes here.

The moment I arrived people from the town opposite started walking across the dry lake bed towards the hotel, which is in the middle of nowhere, and now there is a steady stream shuffling up and down the stairs, opening and closing my door, and at this very moment six people are in my room staring at me. I am virtually trapped in my bed, for under the blankets I have nothing on (with my knees raised, I form a sort of tent, inside which I can at least write in private) and my clothes are in a closet on the other side of the room. Soon I shall either have to shock them or die.

From some two dozen suitcases and trunks standing in a row in the sumptuous lobby, I assumed that I was neither the first nor only guest, but it turns out that I am both, that is, the first and only ever. The baggage belongs to the heiress who never arrived before the war. (Perhaps these spectators have confused notions as to who I am.) How can I stay in this place—indeed, how can I even get out? The manager is a heap of white bones and a rumpled blue suit lying putridly behind the reception desk. I rang the little bell once. Dead for years. His living son, however, is a nice fellow, has promised me a chicken for dinner.

Stuck in my tent as I am, I will relate the toilet: every voyage has its little closet disasters which, in the last analysis, should not be suppressed, for to do so is to falsify and deceive. I mentioned previously that I was suffering from constipation, hence was struck with joy upon seeing a modern bathroom across the hall from my room. I entered and sat and tried to ignore the toilet seat's splitting under my weight—I merely cast it aside. I did manage to ease myself. After four days it was quite a thing. I have no shame in talking about bodily functions (though I never have before). After all, the distance between the head and other parts of the body is but two and a half feet. Considered on a cosmic scale, what is two and a half feet? But the toilet began to crumble under my very self. Such a thing had never happened before. I reached for the chain, now was clinging to it, indeed, dangling from it as the toilet crashed from sight and all the change in my pockets and the floor dropped away in great chunks, and the sink and the bathtub, until my weight ripped the water closet from the wall, and I too plunged. But by some miracle I escaped the fall unharmed, now found myself standing in a large dark hole, some ten feet below where the floor had been, and I will *not* describe it.

I climbed out.

The manager's living son has since tied a roll of toilet paper to the door. A treacherous arrangement: you open the door to a sheer drop of ten feet.

✦

They have finally finished and left. I can see them trekking back across the dry lake from my window. The manager's living son informed me that they were the municipal council, who have (through him) ordered me to take away the heiress's twenty-one pieces of luggage when I leave. I cannot think why, nor did I ask. He's bringing the suitcases up to my room, one by one, a noisy and lengthy process since he's using the elevator, which must be recharged with fresh gunpowder after each usage. I have the tape recorder on. He complains of the weight, saying they must contain books. But the exercise might be good for him. In his slightly disreputable appearance, his sandy hair and green eyes, I detect a capacity for infinite sloth.

✦

I wilt with exhaustion. There is a huge crack developing in the wall. The manager's living son, the heiress's twenty-first piece of luggage and the elevator are missing, and I have been running around the lobby trying to catch that chicken, and am near starving again. I must think clearly. And trap that chicken.

✦

No need. It laid a double-yolk egg in a bamboo planter and I made myself a superb omelette. What I call resourceful traveling. Now I shall go to bed, against speculations on what is inside the heiress's twenty pieces of luggage.

✦

I would like to leave this morning but despair of finding anyone who really wants to go somewhere. Everyone is gone. And I cannot leave alone with all this luggage. Breakfast was odd, definitely odd. I went downstairs at dawn and with friendly clucking sounds tried to commission another egg from the chicken, but to no avail. Then I discovered a telephone behind the desk (cemetery, rather) and was going to call for—*help*, I suppose, in spite of the language difficulty—when the telephone receiver began to melt in my hand, melt, I repeat—for it was made out of a very flavorful chocolate. This was more than enough. It might well be that most of this hotel is edible, that I could stay here virtually forever, or at least until I *became* the Famôus Lake Grand Hotel and had to move on.

Elsewhere, perhaps above, I have refused to refer to what was under the modern bathroom floor. This was a mistake. What value will these notes have if they are not comprehensive from the very beginning?

Under the floor which collapsed was a room identical in every respect, down to the last detail, including *my* traveling things, to the room I am lying in right now.

Which has been described.

I must get out of this place.

✦

There was nothing to do but walk to the town in search of transportation. Before the hotel a grassy slope extended down to the white shoreline of the Famôus Lake which, as seen from the hotel, was dry, that is, a brown lake bed, but as seen directly from the shoreline was filled with water lukewarm to the touch. Thus I was obliged to walk around the lake to the town, twice as far as expected, where I hoped to be recognized if not welcomed by the municipal council who had spent so much time examining me and my personal effects. Though I was in some fear of being seen without the heiress's twenty pieces of luggage which I had been ordered to take with me. Yet how could I carry all that on foot? During the hour's walk it became apparent that the lake was some sort of mirage, that is, an effect. Sadly this was not taken into account during the choice of the hotel site.

Upon reaching the central square of that dull provincial town under the shadow of a very high and startlingly purple mountain range, I wondered what to do next, for the municipal council was nowhere to be seen. I neither spoke the language, had a map, nor any more cash than the equivalent of three dollars; moreover, I knew tales of tourists going begging in the streets of this region. So I passed some time cultivating eye-contact with a large crowd which had been gathered, now cupped my hands to my mouth and shouted for all to hear: *'Does anyone speak English here?'*

I thought I heard behind me a low voice saying slowly, distinctly, 'We all speak English, you fool.' But then I was suffering from indigestion. Incredible flatulations!

A young man detached himself from the hubbub of the central square and introduced himself as a linguist of sorts. What, he asked through a thick accent, could he do for me? I explained that I wished to hire a car to proceed over the mountains to the capital. He replied, how fortunate, he too intended to go to the capital, yet sadly there were no cars of any sort to be hired here, no transportation whatsoever, this being the effect of recent domestic turmoil. Everyone wanted to go to the capital, yet no one could. This was impossible, I replied. I had a letter of introduction to a cabinet minister which I carried in my coat pocket, and told him so. The young linguist of sorts stared at me an instant, then said that in that case, by all means, we should go straight to the municipal museum.

We set off. The linguist of sorts told me that though the domestic turmoil had originated in the capital, the form it took here was a dispute over what the Famôus Lake really was, whether it was one thing or another, wet or dry, and so on. He, my present guide, was the only person left in town who firmly believed that the lake was filled with water or some liquid, and asked me not to abuse that confidence. I told him of course not, for I happened to agree with him.

Though, in a way, I wondered what it really mattered. At the door of the municipal museum, a small stone building of an ancient style, the young linguist of sorts advised me that he had best do all the talking. Did I mind? No, of course not. In that case he would tell the museum director that I was something of a collector of art objects, and if we were lucky we might get away with what we wanted. He told me, in a low voice, that the museum director was a member of the municipal council. Which meant he was a member of the opposition. We went inside.

The museum possessed only one exhibit: a large golden coach. On one of the four red plush seats inside it sat the museum director, literally twiddling his thumbs. (I was told later that he was wondering, as he had been for many years, what to do with the thing.) The young linguist of sorts tapped on the glass and the director looked up and smiled and now stepped out, whereupon I bought two tickets. We all climbed back inside. The seats were sublimely comfortable. The director looked me over carefully, appearing to recognize me, though I could not remember his face from the day before; and now the young man set about explaining my needs. He must have embroidered our agreed-upon deception at length, for he talked on a good half-hour, while the director sighed, coughed, patted me on the shoulder, now slapped his hands on his knees and offered me one to shake. I shook it. (I later found a wad of chewing gum adhering to my palm.)

It was now time to demonstrate the golden coach. The director, knowing I didn't understand his language, exaggerated the gestures accordingly. The squeeze bulb to blow the horns held by three gilded cherubim on the rooftop. The secret button to open the valuables cabinet. The smoking kit's flint-and-tinder lighter. The window pull tassels. And the hand brake.

Upon stepping from the coach, the young linguist of sorts said I was to write out a check for an amount which, considering the rates of exchange, seemed quite modest. He also said to me that obviously I would need something to pull my new find to my distant collection, wouldn't I? Of course. For there was no sense in owning it here while my collection was there. Of course not. He winked at me and turned to the director and explained, at equal length, this new problem.

I could see that the director, from his many frowns and pursings of the lips, feared he would be involved in a transportation plot, or the appearance of one, both equally dangerous to his official position on the municipal council. It also occurred to me—because the director, this time, was not only listening but arguing as well—that the golden coach might have been sold many times before, but never actually carried off, for it was clear that transportation was a subversive word in this town. Grasping this, I interrupted my guide and told him to tell the director (true or not) that I was but a simple tourist who naturally wanted to carry off the choice souvenir I had just bought, and if there was nothing to pull it with I would regrettably have to take it apart and send it through the mail, piece by piece. The young linguist of sorts translated all this, but told me that there was no mail service here. Then I would carry it piece by piece myself over to the hotel and then decide what to do with it.

Perhaps this argument, or another, swayed the museum director, who now led us out the back door to a spacious garden where he swore the young man to secrecy. It seemed that he was the cultivator of an unusual species of white elephant—as were, in truth, most of the townspeople, though no one admitted to this hobby in public. Thus, if he sold us an elephant, would we please be so kind as to never tell where we had bought it? Of course. For if anyone ever found out, he would lose his job, his position on the municipal council, and most likely be exiled or thrown in jail.

Yet, beyond that, we would actually be doing him a service, for he had on his hands an elephant which he needed badly to dispose of but until now had not found the means. One did not simply throw them out on the street, as we knew. That would risk exposure. He now produced the elephant. Clearly it was strong enough to pull the coach. I asked the young man to find out what was wrong with it. The director explained that it was suffering from acne, as we could see, and he had long since despaired of trying to cure it. To make matters worse, some prankster or jealous fellow-cultivator had broken in one night and scribbled dirty words all over its underbelly with indelible ink. Which of course should not bother me since I did not understand the language. I agreed. So we would be doing him a real service to take it off his hands, he would give it to us for nothing if we promised to keep forever secret where we had got it. Of course.

I had many questions at this point but feared that to ask them would mean delaying our departure, which I imagined would be complicated. But no. Neither of them showed any nervousness about moving the white elephant out in the street, a thing which had never been done before in this town; and the crowd which had been gathered out there seemed far more intent upon entering the museum than watching us harness the elephant. To see the new exhibit, the young man remarked. My check. And with some bitterness he added that they would flock to see it in droves. Excusing himself, of course, for belittling something which had come from my own hand. I said I didn't mind.

We set off. Once out of town, the young linguist of sorts commented that we were probably safe now. The very audacity of our escape, he thought, had saved us from being arrested for transportation. I said I didn't understand. Because, he explained, we had become the talk of the town.

✧

Given our agreement about the contents of the Famôus Lake, we went around it, not across, on our way back to the hotel to pick up my suitcase and the heiress's twenty pieces of luggage, at the sight of which the young man laughed. Yes, he said, the municipal council had been trying to get rid of them for the longest time though they had never bothered to see what was inside. Books, probably, the suitcases were things which contained books, whereas most books contained things, which brought up the interesting question of whether there was a book which was also a thing, and a thing which was a book—inseparably, which contained no other thing but itself. I thought not, but said I didn't think the question was all that interesting. And so we carried the suitcases, nicely matched in green leather with gold fittings, down to the coach in silence.

The elephant was a slow walker. Yet no one was pursuing us, reported my companion from frequent backward glances, and soon we were climbing the mountains, which rise higher on this particular continent than elsewhere, and I commend them to the viewing tourist. Who will see, halfway up, the magnificent display of the Famôus Lake, The Famôus Lake, the long narrow valley, or, if he chooses to look upwards, pointed snowy peaks wrapped in clever mists, the soarings of huge birds across crag-hinted voids, a high land, which we now reached and where vegetation grew sparse or not at all except for a small blue flower that sat atop fence posts, though it too may have been a bird.

Now that we were safely out of town, indeed, almost all civilization, for no one at all seemed to live amongst this harsh scenery, the young linguist of sorts began to speak with some confidence upon a variety of subjects, which he intermingled in a pleasant way to reach the startling conclusion that he was bent upon filling all the world's ears and books and then some, and that he would not rest until he had convinced me, convinced every rock, stone, peak and thing. Of what? I could not be sure. For suddenly he was silent. Actually he was not as young as all that: about my age. I will not dwell on other points of resemblance, which were innumerable. And now he turned to the scenery, pulling me over by the cuff to see the magnificent display of the Famôus Lake, The Famôus Lake, the long narrow valley, while above us he pointed out how anxious mists danced before snowy peaks and huge birds slashed the voids above or beside a rocky earth barren of almost all, but not quite all, vegetation.

Which, of course, I had already seen.

After another long silence the young man said that now that we were out of earshot of the others he could confess openly that he was going to the capital with a special purpose. Meaning? Meaning, he said, that back at home he had embarked on the project of inventing just one new word, which had led him into inventing a whole world—and he had almost botched it up. I was not surprised. I asked him for what new thing he had invented the word to describe, and he replied that he had invented the word first, so as to invent the thing next. That was how he got started. And, of course, once you started—if you could—what was to be believed thereafter? Or worse, who would believe you? So he was going on for a fresh start to the capital, whose citizens would be less narrow-minded than those of his provincial home and where he hoped he might be able to complete his work. Or if not there, somewhere farther on.

But I wanted to know about this word. He said that since it had caused him so much trouble he had given it up and even managed to forget it. Then he leaned over to me and said that if he mentioned it now, even whispered it into my ear, and if I understood it, if I saw its thing, everything else would start falling to pieces, bit by bit, and we would never reach the capital, for in the other words that might spring from it, the capital would cease to be, and we stranded nowhere at all. I could not but praise his now tactful silence. He added that he had learned his lesson: that although inventing just one new word might seem easy, one had to be careful, for the dangers were legion.

I quite agreed.

That was why, in short, the municipal council had ordered him to leave town. Ordered him? Yes, he said, ordered. And he wished to apologize for having involved me in a web of deception, as perhaps I might have wanted to stay there a little longer myself. Not at all. But back there he could have hardly admitted to me that he was the only member of the town not on the municipal council, and that he had been asked to leave although also denied any means of transportation out. I said I was quite happy to have saved him from his incredible circumstances, but couldn't see why they had wanted him to leave. Because, he said, he was not on the municipal council.

This, for him, seemed to be the final argument, clear and self-evident, the product of some local peculiarity which I might never understand.

And, he added after a time, the municipal council did not like his word. I was astounded that he had actually shown it to them. Yes, he said, that was some time ago. They hadn't known quite what to do with it, so they had decided to have it sent to the capital to see what they thought of it. And had this been done? Yes, so to speak, he replied. The municipal council had had the word engraved on the head of a pin so that it could not be casually read off, and then by a series of incredible mishaps, the pin got dropped into a huge pile of hay inside a boxcar with ten starving horses, all bound for the capital. That is, they said it was all by accident. But he was not convinced. So that was another reason he was going to the capital, to try to recover his word.

I wished him luck.

But he answered my remark with a grim silence, so I turned

again to examine the view, which was as before though smaller and somewhat fogged and graced now with the blur of a person to the other side of the road, a woman standing in a hitch-hiking pose, bound for the opposite direction. I stopped the coach and pulled down my window. At that she saw us and crossed the cold rough ground to engage us in conversation. (She appeared to be the Païnted Wōman.) Although coming from the capital, she claimed, she was much in need of a ride in any direction owing to the intense cold. Her skirt, of a deep lavender and heavy of material, was probably adequate for the climate, though her blouse, a thin thing patterned in chilly blues, suggested better how cold she was than any shiverings and chatterings of teeth would ever have done. Traffic, she added, was sparse or nonexistent. Night was apt to fall soon.

She held through all this, in spite of the cold, in spite of her rapid speech, a smile so long and steady that it seemed she was trying to rack up some curious statistic.

Of course the problem was simple, indeed, elementary. She was really going in one direction and I in another, so that if she came along she would be advancing her travels not one inch; on the contrary, she would be doing them positive harm, which might well engage the rest of us in a great deal of needless suffering. The possibility of her corrupting the young linguist of sorts was not all that distant. In which case I should have to ask them both to leave. As an intolerable situation. I am a professional traveler and must take certain precautions. Or there was simply no room in the coach. But none of this did I say to her: so compactly was it all stored in the monosyllabic 'no' which I uttered, or in the elaborate intonations woven into the very mouthing of it, a brief explosive report, not unlike, in these wastes, a muffled gunshot.

We continued on our way.

The young linguist of sorts, with unseemly anxiety, wanted to know who she was.

'My wife,' I said with a laugh.

But after a time my annoyance faded, for I reflected that perhaps she had been wondering who I was. She might not have seen. Indeed the mist had become a virtual fog, obscuring even the white snow which lay all around us, permitting only the occasional glint of a deep-blue glacier to penetrate, and all sense of panorama was soon gone, and the road was threatened, our path. So we halted to collect our bearings. This being the first level stretch in hours, very possibly we had reached the summit. We stepped outside, and it was cold. Sending the young man off to explore, I stayed with the coach and held a firm hand on one of its knobs so as to avoid the risk of losing everything. He was back in a flash to announce that he had practically walked into the side of an enormous beige tent where we were invited to spend the night, though he thought it advisable to leave the white elephant Unable (loose translation of his name by way of a number of ancillary languages) parked outside.

Thus, by way of a zippered flap, we entered the tent. Which appeared to be filled with several hundred mountain goats of a sort I have never seen before and which gave off a sweet, cloying perfume that was almost palpable, of a stickiness. The hair, the animals' hair, long and whiter than the finest of snows, was braided towards the floor and festooned with ribbons, bells, foil, wire and something resembling automobile reflectors, and other things, while the eyes were fitted with fashionable dark glasses, perhaps protection against the white hair or snow, or both. From the advantage of my height, I could see that the eyes were of the finest of blues, hard and geometric. As for the horns, each goat possessed a single coil or spiral, festively hung with what looked like color pages from opulent magazines and tipped with a variety of rubber stoppers destined to prevent the tent-fabric, which was quite low to the ground in spots, from being punctured during their perambulations.

They communicated with each other in the usual fashion. That is, by word of mouth.

The young man now introduced the goatherds, who were not readily distinguishable. At first sight they appeared to be only simpler goats, but after a time I noticed that they were afflicted with a tic-like gesture for raising up their dark glasses, and that their goat-skins were entirely unadorned. There might have been a half-dozen, all men, of startlingly golden hair, sandy at the sideburns. A handsome race, though clearly in the throes of a degeneration. Their green eyes were most shifty, most erratic.

Offered a pair of nest-like seats, the young man and I sat down to an eye-level of hundreds of dark glasses. (I was never able to determine the source of an even, pure light which illuminated the tent until exactly midnight.) The young man now related the history of this suburban tribe. We were but twenty miles from the capital. Where he found all this out, I don't know. But the gist was that the goatherds, a monastic sect, had long ago in the past viewed the goats as incarnate divinities, but now, under certain influences, were beginning to realize that a goat, after all, might just be a goat. This uninterrupted worship had unfortunately turned the goatherds, a once-proud nomadic tribe, into semi-invalids whose lives were now consumed in interminable tent-weaving and hair-grooming. The important point was, however, that it would have been unwise to bring the white elephant into the tent.

Frankly I do not see any of this.

And suspect that the whole tent was the work of the linguist of sorts. Had he, perhaps unawares, let slip that word of his? But I could not risk the asking.

Dinner was served in the form of a white mush or mash the likes of which I have never tasted before and so cannot describe, and afterwards our host came around and offered us each a small cylinder, some three inches long and the diameter of, say, an ordinary cigarette, stuffed with something resembling tobacco. One end of the thing was to be put in the mouth while the other was illuminated by a torch passed around the tent. A bluish-white gas was produced upon ignition; when breathed it brought on the most powerful of visions, lacking however in a certain noteworthy quality, for after studious comparisons the visions proved to be exactly identical to what one was actually seeing, or would have seen free of the effects of the drug.

I took advantage of this unexpected lull to slip on my parachute-orange bathrobe, very light of material, which I prefer to relax in.

At the crack of dawn, or at the very moment the upper chip of sun sprayed the horizon with a blinding glare, we emerged from the tent to find our elephant frozen solid. The young man explained that this was inclined to happen, but promised that if we dedicated the morning to artfully massaging it we would surely reach the capital by nightfall.

Once again he turned out to be right.

✦

In spite of its situation the capital is very chic. Filled with notable monuments, buildings, exhibits, affairs, activities, trade, cultures, which you can find adequately described and illustrated in the handy reference works at your local public library which indeed should be your companion to this volume.

The young man's instinctive knowledge of the capital brought us to the cabinet minister's front gate where, with many fond wishes for mutual success, we parted ways.

I am working in bed now. This door has a solid slide latch on it. A small but important feature which spares me countless interruptions and keeps me from losing my mind. The cabinet minister means well, I am sure. His hospitality is nothing less than national. His mansion, the largest I have ever seen, is decorated in the charming capitoline manner, half of it at least, the only half I have seen. He has a wife and seven children (whom I have not met).

I said I wished to spend the morning resting up.

That I did not want to be disturbed any more.

The tape recorder, purchased on a previous trip around the world, is proving to be a more limited device than hoped. Such a machine, which records all sound indiscriminately, can only fit, I see now, a situation in which all sound can be controlled or, as it were, be made to perform; and this would mean throwing the raw, brute moment right out the window.

I will give it another try some day. Rest and relaxation today. Tomorrow I will do some sightseeing on the way to the bank where I must go to cash a check so I can pay off my debts. Only the wealthy are advised to accept invitations from the cabinet minister. I am wealthy. Very. I hope to meet him soon. He must be a charming man, of undeniable administrative genius. I was met at the front gate by a crowd of people all clamoring for my letter of introduction, and who it was that finally carried it off I am not sure. A family reunion? Political gathering? Secret police? Then, as I was just about to write off the visit as ill-timed and set off in search of a hotel, there was a rush to carry my baggage into the mansion, and I was told to follow on the double and was pushed and pulled from here to there. These people, all thirty of them men, were dressed in a curious diversity ranging from a full tuxedo to what can only be called a loin-cloth—or less.

One of them could well have been the cabinet minister. Who, from newspaper photographs, appears to have a bone structure similar to my own.

I was put in the guest room and left alone there for several hours to the sound of a great thundering outside the door. I was afraid either to lock it or venture outside, and so sat on the bed between apprehension and expectation. That I should be asked to leave or that I should be paid a personal visit of welcome by the cabinet minister himself. At last the door opened and a fellow came in wearing a white linen suit similar but not identical to my own. He was not the cabinet minister. In broken English he informed me that he had just volunteered for the post of my servant and, if unoccupied, he would be glad to accept the position. But there was something extraordinarily familiar about the fellow, something which the cut of his hair, the suit seemed to obscure. Then I laughed. He was none other than the young linguist of sorts! Small world! I asked him what on earth he was doing here. We shook hands warmly and he explained. No sooner had he left me than he perceived that he was almost penniless and that there would be little hope of going through with his plans in that state; he would need to work awhile and earn some money, and then see. So he had gone around to the mansion's service entrance and applied for a job. The cabinet minister's personnel manager told him that something might be opening up that very moment, and so he was given a brief but rigorous training course—and here he was. I congratulated him for his quick success and said, as far as I was concerned, he could choose between being my servant and my valet. The former, he preferred. And so I hired him on the spot. He thanked me, adding that unfortunately he was pledged to secrecy concerning many aspects of the household and if I would be so kind as not to ask, he would be greatly relieved. Of course. Now he said that I was to avail myself of his services for anything I wished, and if he might offer a suggestion, it would be appropriate for me to send him off to the cabinet minister bearing expressions of my gratitude for his lavish hospitality, along with any other greetings I might have. I said that was an excellent idea; he left. I decided not to be affronted at this curious custom. Not yet. It was too early. A while later he returned with a number of other people, probably part of the crowd at the door, and translated their remarks—that the cabinet minister was delighted to have me as a guest; that the cabinet minister wished me to feel at home; that the cabinet minister would consider it an honor to be able to do anything in his power to make my visit to the capital a pleasant one; that the cabinet minister was delighted to meet me. I replied to my servant that I was charmed with the guest room and quite certain I would have a pleasant stay in the capital, and he left again with the other people to convey my remarks to the cabinet minister.

Now I understood. All these people were the cabinet minister's servants. And even: one of them might have been the cabinet minister himself.

But the formalities were not over. Soon the cabinet minister's wife unleashed a horde of servants on me, and I could not count them all, and I had to dispatch my poor servant half a dozen times to satisfy her demands for compliments. Then came the innumerable servants of the cabinet minister's seven children, sullen and ill-behaved characters who had only one thing in mind. I whispered to my servant that I had nothing to give them for their young masters, and he winked and unlocked a closet filled with candies and toys, and suggested which would make the best presents. I sent him off with an armload of terribly expensive things and got in return not one word of thanks. (Excluding, perhaps, a dead bird which someone tossed in the door while my back was turned.) And someone made a profit on that transaction—probably the little bastards themselves.

Here, on the contrary, there was no question that any of these servants could have been the cabinet minister's wife or children, for they were all full-grown men, quite full-grown, underneath their women's and children's clothes, underneath their affected manners and moods. And I assume that the painting in the dining room of a nude woman reclining in a bed of blue flowers is in reality a portrait of the cabinet minister's wife. A pretty thing, but sadly marred by a flowing mustache, the product no doubt of some vandal. However an expert is at work restoring it.

Now followed several hours during which the servants combined forces to stage re-enactments in my room of what my hosts were doing in the other part of the mansion. This cost me a fortune. Finally I told my servant I wanted to rest, could he please get them to leave. Now he is sitting in a corner answering the phone—it rings continuously—in a manner so discreet I am hardly bothered at all by his presence. And financially, it has been a windfall, or rather an economy, since when the cabinet minister's servants telephone there is no way to tip them.

Fortunately the guest room is much less opulent than the rest of the mansion, which is as I prefer. The bed, being hard, allows me to work on my notes for hours on end without fatigue and did I so wish I would be able to stay in it for days, not even having to avail myself of the handsome desk or writing table opposite, whose thin legs support the solid top, perhaps of walnut, as if by levitation; it contains a solitary lockable drawer, and there is a matching chair with a sort of wicker seat. Where my servant now sits, attending to the telephone. The blue carpet, which does not quite cover the hardwood floor, has a nice glow to it and the tone matches one of the shades, or perhaps a mixture of several, in the curiously patterned blue wallpaper, chosen I suspect by the cabinet minister's wife or one of her servants. But I am especially delighted by the bare globe in the center of the ceiling: I prefer this sort of lighting to desk and table lamps for the peculiar celestial effect, and am fond of strong shadows, which this one does indeed cast.

My servant, however, keeps shading his eyes against the glare. Well, he will get used to it.

My only complaint is that in order to reach the bathroom, which is in fact next door, one must go by way of the hall, with all that implies.

✧

At the advice of one of the cabinet minister's servants, I went to the Black Bank this afternoon on foot in order to see some of the capital which, with its tree-lined boulevards, smartly dressed citizens and many tall buildings, as set beneath a towering mountain range, is impressive beyond words, and I cannot recommend it too highly for those who like cities. It seems that the capital is now in the grips of domestic turmoil, and the cabinet minister, fearing I might be molested, ordered three of his servants to escort me. I protested but am not armed. I could only command my servant to stay at home. Indeed there were a few unruly mobs roaming around the central squares, up to no good—what?—although the cabinet minister's servants refused all comment while whisking me towards the most central of squares, where I glimpsed one incident—a woman giving public birth to a child. (They did not know I saw that.) It would be utter folly to say that her face, so contorted with pain, looked familiar.

Happily the servants left me at the door of the Black Bank so that I might carry out my transactions with the privacy that is so hard to come by around here. The interior of the bank is beyond words on account of the dim lighting provided by only three carbide lamps, which hiss from fluted pillars. The very high vaulted ceiling is the oldest in the capital. In order to see it, the tourist is advised to come equipped with a flashlight. After standing around a moment just inside the entrance, I was taken by someone I couldn't make out too clearly to a wooden booth with a stool in it and told to go inside. The door closed upon me. I sat down in the stuffy, cramped darkness and waited for an indeterminate time. Abruptly an unctuous voice to one side asked how much money I wanted. I lit a match. To the right of my head was a wooden grille of many small hand-carved holes, through which I could see nothing but more darkness. I stated the amount in dollars. A long silence. Then, after a racking cough, the voice asked whether I was an honest man. Or whether I was not a dishonest man. The accent was very thick. I replied that that was not for me to judge. Did I have an honest face, at least? Frankly, I said, when I looked at myself in the mirror, I thought I had an honest face, but this was a strictly personal opinion. There was a windy sigh, and then the voice asked, with a note of exasperation, whether perhaps I was not at this very moment concealing my face behind a handkerchief, whether I was not holding a gun in one hand and a paper sack in the other. I said of course not. Suddenly there was some scuffling around the back of the partition, followed by a dull thud at my very feet, and the door swung open at last, letting in a little light. I groped around with my hands and picked up a large paper sack. Inside was a pistol and a rubber mask whose features I could not make out in the gloom. Then the voice said between coughs, which soon exploded into awful retching sounds, that I was to take these things to the manager.

I stepped outside quickly, to find myself in the custody of a boy on a tricycle with a small lamp on the handlebars. He led me across a rough stone floor towards the far end of the interior. It seemed that I was the only client. Large insects and small rodents scurried across the lamp's dim beam. We soon arrived, as I was to learn later, at the world's largest drawing of a bank vault door, where the little boy sounded his bell and then rode away. Through the drawing, which was on a very fine bluish paper and which extended the width and height of the building, I heard what might have been an invitation to come in. I considered at length how this could be done, and in the end employed a fingernail, cutting a relatively smooth line, through which I slid.

I found myself standing before an old man at a roll-top desk piled high with thick volumes, and to whom I gave up the paper sack with the pistol and the mask still inside. He seemed to be very glad to see me. But I could not tell, because he did not speak English. However, gestures soon sufficed and we passed a most agreeable time thumbing through currency catalogues to select engraving patterns, colors, types of paper, watermarks, sizes and denominations. Then he called in the head engraver, who made a rapid but flawless engraving of my semi-profile poised upon an athletic, muscular body heaving something like a javelin. He indicated he could add a fig leaf if I desired, but I thought I might as well live it up and said no. In the last analysis it wasn't mine anyway. He went off for a time to do the printing, and when the results were ready—a large carton with bank notes in all the specifications I had requested—he slipped me also, compliments of the house, a heavy sack of coins on which I was most pleased to discover my likeness as well. I gathered he had struck them while waiting for the ink to dry.

I thanked them both and wandered back through the gloom to the main entrance. Outside I discovered that a passing riot had carried off one of the cabinet minister's servants. Which one, I could not be sure.

✦

The young man who became my servant seems to be undergoing a slow transformation. Yesterday, I believe I mentioned, he put on a white linen suit similar to mine. Since then he has found one which is identical. I pretend not to notice any of this. What he does with his time is none of my business. However, I cannot avoid noticing his new light-blue tie, black socks, gold monogrammed cufflinks and patent leather shoes which are also the very same as mine. And he is taking up but has not mastered a gesture that I picked up somewhere on my travels: a slow twirling movement of the right hand while talking, such as one might use in setting the hands of a large clock. And if I am not mistaken he is losing weight. Odd.

The cabinet minister has invited me to see the capital by night, that is, one of his servants has, and I have sent off mine to accept. Surely this will be the chance to meet him. His servants are generally likable. But hers and the children's are intolerable—grown men dressing up as women and children and romping, screaming, weeping through the interminable halls of this mansion, between my room and theirs, all day long ...

Whatever possessed me to force the lock on one of the heiress's twenty pieces of luggage?

Of course: I have no key.

✦

The cabinet minister remains inaccessible, elusive, aloof, and I did not even *see* him last night and now begin to wonder what the devil he is up to. I have nothing to give him beyond what I have given him: a letter of introduction. What else does he want? What else could I possibly give him?

My servant's English is not yet up to dealing with this complicated situation, but in time ...

Last night the servants were most elegantly dressed, over twenty-five of them in seven automobiles, and to the wail of sirens we rushed through the picturesque streets of the entertainments quarter, that is, the section of it which has not yet been engulfed in the domestic turmoil. Dinner upon the rarest of indescribable delicacies in a subterranean restaurant—the cabinet minister is believed to have eaten down the street—with a liberal quantity of the local alcoholic beverage which I drank far too much of. My servant was at my side most of the evening, his studious eye constantly upon me. Frankly I had little to say to the cabinet minister's second-hand table talk. His servants were disgracefully drunk. The cabinet minister (therefore) was even more disgracefully drunk. Drunker even than I.

I should say that the dinner would have been agreeable, perhaps, had his servants been interesting as individuals, which they are not. A situation very unhealthy as far as the servants go, for they are drained of all character or personality beyond those scraps borrowed from their master, who uses them as personal extensions of himself, almost mechanical. I imagine they must undergo an elaborate (and demoralizing) training course, in which they constantly observe their master in whatever situation or mood they are hired to convey; equally, the cabinet minister must select men with subtle powers of observation, but men who are, in one respect or another, either weaker or less clever than he. Otherwise, what would prevent a servant, after this arduous course of imitation, from taking over and wresting power from the cabinet minister?

But I deplore the human loss, which has tragic aspects on both sides: the servants are not only exploited, but the cabinet minister's curious personality also is but loosely conveyed by his servants, even when they are all assembled; and so the cabinet minister is not served, not truly described, except in terms of an inner void, left by that which the servants, no matter how hard they work, can never convey, singly or together.

Nor can I be sure that this is what his servants are for. My narrow experience—one servant, and a good fellow at that—is inadequate for such generalizations, but it would seem, if rumor is to be believed, that the cabinet minister needs all these servants because he is something of an invalid, and cannot get around. Yet the same rumor has it that he is an invalid by choice, that is, he does not want to get around.

I shall not know what to make of this until, if ever, I meet the man.

After dinner there came a brief visit to the national bordello, a charming place which I endorse with my hearty recommendations. According to my servant, the building is a converted music hall, a fact which tasteful redecoration completely conceals. The solitary woman of pleasure, nude and reclining, measures some ninety feet from head to foot; assembled out of a very soft plastic by a foreign aircraft producer, it or she should be added to the list of wonders of the world without further delay. Contains only one moving part; tickets to it (ask for the reduced tourist rate) are dispensed from a little booth at the thigh, from which one proceeds to an underground dressing room and then mounts a very narrow staircase. There one will have one's money's worth without question. Afterwards you may ascend to a circular gallery fitted with comfortable loges with an excellent view of the entire figure from above. I sat some time up there with my servant. We both came away with the feeling that the mammoth plastic face was familiar, perhaps very familiar. I don't know what's the matter with *him*.

Beyond that, the entertainments are such as you would find in any large city worthy of the name.

The noise outside my door is intolerable.

I am resting up from last night.

⁂

The things I found in the suitcase repel. They repel in all directions. Why? Is it the horror of unwanted antiquity? Or the collisions of two seemingly separate passages of time? They were: seven masonite panels painted white and bearing in thick black letters archaic words referring to things which no longer exist; or words found in every brain but now obsolete and useless, like the appendix, tonsils, body hair and toenails. Neither wanting to keep the panels, which are distasteful, displeasing and awful, nor knowing exactly how to throw them away, I have slipped them between the mattress and springs of the bed I now lie upon, hoping thus to cure a backache. The bed sags less now though every once in a while—whenever I make a sudden movement—one of the panels cracks.

Time is a ridiculous concept. Nevertheless the next day or the next week—or why not be lavish or simply truthful? The next decade?—my wrath at the ruckus or rumpus the cabinet minister's servants were kicking up outside my door at all hours of the day and night reached such a point that I became unshakably determined for once and for all to meet the man who was my charming and affable host (according to the servants) in order to register my disapproval in person and clear away this domestic red tape, which was costing me lost hours, great sums in tips and threatening nervous disorders to which I am not normally prone. I must now speak of the astonishing transformation my servant had undergone. He so resembled me that now we were virtually indistinguishable. The same clothes; the same square, bony stature; the same green eyes; the same long reddish-gold hair parted down the middle; the same sensitively dissipated face (a dark wash under the eyes); the same rather halting manner of speaking; and in fact my servant had even managed to eradicate his thick accent in English—an achievement which caused him to sacrifice much of his own language. Yet, he still had access to the cabinet minister, and now it was simply a matter of changing roles—after a fashion.

Late that morning I ordered my servant to run the bath, and as soon as he left the room I followed him out and down the hall those two or three yards to the bathroom where I locked him in. As an extra precaution I slipped a note under the door that he was not to break it down and try to escape. I had written this out in advance. At this moment the hallway appeared deserted, in the living sense at least, for part of the charming capitoline manner of decoration consists in using the exterior of doors as painting surfaces, most commonly for full-length portraits of past and present residents. So I could not be certain. I went back to the room for a brief nap. Now, a few minutes later, as I stepped into a seemingly interminable distance, at that moment, again it appeared to be utterly deserted. No movement, no sound. But that moment passed, for I had taken but one step down the hallway when the countless portrait doors to either side began opening, and I saw the assembled servants peering out. But they were not looking in my direction; they were staring down the hall, away from me, towards the very end, towards an open doorway at the very end of the hall, and in the doorway, made tiny by the distance, stood a man transfixed by an oblique ray of sunlight, and at that instant I was overcome by the certainty that at last I was looking at *him*, the cabinet minister himself, a certainty not lessened, not at all, by the fact that he was wearing a mask, which I cannot describe. But I knew not whether to advance down the very long hallway towards the tiny masked figure of the cabinet minister—and risk exposure by one of the servants—or whether simply to stand and be satisfied with being able to look at him from a distance; but now, while I was still wavering, another figure appeared in the very distant doorway, of a woman, whom I could not recognize even with all the sunlight upon her face. Now everything happened at once, and only an instant later did I realize I had just seen the strange woman raise her hand and assassinate the cabinet minister with a cherry pie.

A great moan went up from the assembled servants. Some fell on the floor to grovel absently; others ran insanely in all directions; many beat their heads against the very expensive furnishings. Quickly I retreated down the hallway, intending to unlock my servant and leave the mansion at once, but found myself facing a group of soldiers who were assembling a machine gun in the front doorway; two officers, pistols drawn, were shouting down the hall for quiet and immobility, and it was clear that should I proceed farther in the direction of my room or the bathroom I might well be shot. But I had stopped at a door. It was ajar. I flung myself through it with a terrible crash—into a bedroom the same size as my own, but furnished for use by lady-guests, or the cabinet minister's wife. But I did not pause to study the decor. Rather, I picked up a chair and smashed the window, then climbed out into the garden. Its very fine display of flowers and plants was being trampled by other servants going berserk. The long driveway was clogged by military vehicles disgorging more soldiers who behaved in an aimless manner, as if they didn't quite know what they were here for. Perhaps they were awaiting proper orders. But there was no doubt in my mind that the uprising was directed towards my person. This sort of thing happens only once in a lifetime, and it is not pleasant.

I resolved then to leave everything behind and escape. My servant, my luggage, everything. This was a difficult decision. With an air of feigned distraction, I turned and headed towards the rear of the mansion, ambling this way and that, past clusters of wild-eyed servants and on-looking soldiers, through the once well-tended garden, which was most cultivated close to the building, becoming progressively wilder with distance, ending in a tangle of flowering bushes, a strip of almost virgin forest and a rusty iron fence, which I climbed over to gain the residential street that ran back of the property. Where I saw that the uprising seemed to be spreading all over the capital. More soldiers stood on the sidewalks, and everyone seemed to be leaving their houses and cars to walk towards what I thought was the center of town. I could not very well go in the opposite direction without being remarked and perhaps arrested, so I joined them.

We were yet a sparse gathering of pedestrians, tramping on under the careless eyes of the soldiers, and there was something sullen and sluggish about everyone which I dutifully imitated. I feared to ask where we were walking and why, for lack of the proper language. The residential street was most handsome, however, lined as it was with considerable mansions and great shady trees, and I confess to a pleasure at having been able to walk down the middle of it, what with the prohibition of all vehicular traffic. Here and there a family would leave its house and join us, some making a great fuss about locking everything up, others leaving windows and doors wide open, perhaps assuming that when the moment of pillage and plunder came no lock or latch could ever hold, or that the soldiers, who tended to congregate before the more opulent houses, if they could steal freely, might forgo the pleasures of general destruction.

The residential street ended at one of the capital's magnificent radial boulevards, and here we turned right to join a surging flow of people, all heading in one direction, perhaps towards the center; and on we walked, slowly, thirty abreast, in a silence free of even a murmur, beyond the little cries, here and there, of foot accidents. I was indeed tired. At last came a point of blockage, where two oblique lines of soldiers stood across the boulevard in such a way as to funnel us into a single file, into a serpentine line that extended down the center of the boulevard as far as the eye could see. Because we were now in the thousands, it took all afternoon for me to pass through the funnel to the single file, but here, fortunately, refreshments were served.

And I was not recognized.

Night fell upon the line with the sudden way it does in a city, but more sudden this evening as the capital was left in darkness except for a reddish glow, perhaps of lights, in the far distance. An interminable traffic of coughs and grunts passed up and down the line, over the shufflings of thousands of feet which left noise-prints in the deepening blackness like the marks of a weekend crowd on a sandy beach, now deserted. No one spoke. We moved with the thick slowness of a natural process—a tide, a glacier, lava, a movement of ooze. Night did not pass, it lengthened, stretched, as we feasted past darkened buildings. I know each of them. I could build them all in shadow with my bare hands, to the last detail.

The vague reddish lights acquired a glitter.

And their glitter later formed what might have been a movie-house marquee, troubled by waves of body heat rising from the line.

Now we reached the murmur point. I could not understand what was being said softly by the person in front of me, through me, to the person behind. But perhaps they were saying that the end of the line was close. But this I could soon see.

Powerful floodlights illuminated the last few yards of the line and were hung above what seemed to be a wooden desk or table. Behind was the silhouette of a man hunched over a blank sheet of paper, a ballpoint pen, an alarm clock. The system, which I saw with my own eyes: exactly every minute he directed the person at the head of the line to follow a pedestrian crossing to one side of the boulevard, to an alley, to a firing squad. Their rifles had silencers on them. There was no sound above the shuffling of feet, which trailed off behind us now in one-minute waves. Now I was at the counting point. Whether I wanted to or not, I knew exactly how many were ahead of me. One by one. Without word—only the very light *tick!* of the ballpoint pen tapping the wood—my predecessor was sent off. Should one watch or not? No, there was no time, not a minute to lose. Not now. With a judicious admixture of pride and humility I bent forward to see what was on the sheet of paper before the man, I bent forward to make my head pass from the floodlit glare into the more shadowy region surrounding the desk, so that I might present my unblinded naked glance, my unspoken question, my last possession: a twinkling eye. But my gaze was momentarily distracted by a curious thing behind him, a simple unmade bed, where perhaps his tiring job drove him frequently to catnaps, or something; and only then did I begin to see his face, oddly familiar, and my jaws opened to speak—but snapped closed as a voice hissed into my ear, commanding me to say nothing.

Someone grabbed me by the elbow and pulled me away to the left, back into the glare of floodlights, and I stumbled along a few steps, pulled and blinded, before I finally recognized my servant. Quickly, he said, for there was no time to lose. I gasped and thanked him for saving my life. He might have laughed had we not been in the escort of a military delegation carrying a black cushion covered with medals and ribbons, and all my extensive luggage, but instead said through his teeth that there had been no danger since they were only executing the capital's women. Oh. I asked him to explain. And as he whispered, we all walked snappily down a darkened street, turned a corner and entered a great domed building, perhaps the only one illuminated in the capital that night, and from here, in the train waiting inside, my servant indicated that we were to make our escape, for though the situation was in hand at the moment, it was certain to change for the worse before dawn.

During my brief tenure as prime minister—though it was never clear and matters little who exactly was prime minister, I or my servant or both—my contribution to the nation was, frankly, of little significance. The nation was too far gone, and this was not one of those great occasions to which I or any man might easily rise into what is called greatness; and the choice would have been to stay around, clutching at straws, until made a fool. As prime minister, I fear that the nation was unprepared to receive any contribution I might make, even the most carefully designed and brilliant reform. In the end it is perhaps better to succeed at one tiny act than botch up a universal program, and with that in mind I did just one thing: in the great domed hall I confiscated the train and decreed that it should leave at a quarter past the hour in question. I am convinced that this, the only decisive government policy in years, will go down in history as: 'The train left exactly on time.'

✦

Or I was God; and wondered. An uncomfortable position to be in. Until I was no longer God.

But if there still is a god, He is like me. He must be.

✦

We are hiding out in a cottage in the foothills of the purple range. My servant is really a charming fellow. You would think that our being identical would create misunderstandings. On the contrary. We get along perfectly. I have never possessed such a pleasant traveling companion.

And if the truth must transpire, as inevitably it will, my servant and I are having something of an affair. It started quite by accident, seems that in his haste he forgot to pack my pyjamas and they were lost in the revolution, ended up nude in my bed with my servant who of course does everything now exactly the same as I do. We agree about everything. We agree that this little affair, which has been going on steadily for some days now, is a perfectly normal happening between two normally erotic males who are extremely fond of each other, and is the effect of this isolated cottage. We agree that this has never happened before. (I suspect he is not telling the truth.) We talk to each other endlessly. We are certain this minor infatuation will endure forever, in fact we have decided that we are in no hurry at all to continue our escape. Let them come and get us! We care nothing for such paltry things as our lives! To die together would be the finest of all ends, to die by twin bullets against a wall! We worship our bodies and spend hours improving them, using them, honing them like fine and valuable tools. Our everlasting ecstasy has made the keeping of these notes difficult and painful, and I have been able to put down as much as I have only because of my servant's cooperation—he writes one word, he writes one word, I write the next, I write the next, and you see how perfect the results are: utterly indistinguishable from my solitary labors.

We will go around the world together, again and again! What joy!

Using a map of the continent as a target board we have been whiling away the hours playing darts, and the place we will escape to is the one with the most holes in it. (Name now illegible.) We will have to leave soon. This morning before breakfast high-powered bombers strafed and bombed the cottage next door and we were forced to move our love-making under the bed. But things are shaping up. For our escape we have hit upon a clever plan—to disguise ourselves as women! (It was tending towards that anyway!) We broke open another of the heiress's suitcases and found two identical dark skirts (lavender woven over with black) and two flowery blue blouses which fit perfectly. We will have one last candlelight supper this evening and then slink away at the crack of dawn. We are so sad to leave this place! We are almost in tears! And tomorrow they will destroy what would have become a national shrine—our little cottage, the prime ministers' love-nest.

But no, we did not sleep; we danced, we made love all night, and at the first and most dim glimmer of daylight we set off into the forest and felled ten stout trees in the form of our initials and rolled the logs down to the river, where we made a raft so sturdy that it could have carried three times our luggage, or a floating band, or a brace of hardy rowers, or God knows what. After a breakfast of crumbled biscuits, we set sail, we drifted down the meandering river, and while rounding a bend the sun appeared, and there was a roar in the sky, explosions: pebbles and bits of plaster, wood, torn fragments of bedsheets all splashed into the water around us, and our distant cottage was no more—only a gaping hole in the ground, spat at by flashing squadrons of high-powered bombers whose raucous vituperations were as an unwitting measure of the greatness of our love.

It was the most beautiful of all rivers we have seen, and by actual count I have now seen them all, and as the sun grew high we shed our disguises and swam naked, we caught lethargic trout-like fishes with our bare hands in the tepid waters amid thousands of strands of a deep-blue water grass which pointed wavy fingers in the direction of our drift. And our little raft became the center of a fleet or flock or school of brightly plumaged underwater birds who sang in unison the most melodious of songs, but we could not record them because they sang only underwater, a tune we have never heard but shall never forget. Every now and then they would poke their straw-like beaks through the silvery surface of water, now flit playfully around the underside of the raft, amongst whose wet branches they sought, it seemed, a place to nest. And when we grew tired of watching these underwater antics, we surfaced, we climbed up on the raft, we threw ourselves down to sunbathe, adding two proud masts to our tiny ship.

The wide and slow river flowed through the thickest of forests at the base of the sheerest of high canyon walls, which measured perhaps some thousands of feet up; yet because of the time of day we were never in the shade, and it seemed so sad that this day too must come to an end.

Which I must now describe.

Later in the afternoon we were roused from drowsy embraces by the sound of a distant motor, such as might be attached to a small boat. We disentangled our bronzed limbs and sat up. The noise grew louder. We slipped on the skirts and blouses and now, as we were rounding a lazy bend, a small speedboat appeared, skimming upriver towards us. Soon it passed. At the controls was an attractive young man dressed in a natty white suit who, upon seeing us, shut down the motor and began circling around us at a slower speed. We waved. He hailed us. We were undoubtedly an impressive, if not touching, sight. Slowly he drew his small metal boat towards the raft, closer and closer, until he reached out to grab a branch. The gesture—that wrist—revealed one small troubling thing—and now I saw. He was not a young man at all: he, she was a woman disguised as one. Now. And she saw now that we were not women, and I recognized her and she me.

Nonetheless—this was my mistake—we invited her on

board. She explained that she was fleeing upriver from domestic upheavals in the country we were escaping to and which, according to her, we were already in, having crossed the frontier some miles back. I was beginning to feel uneasy in the skirt and blouse, no longer necessary, so I excused myself and went to the other side of the raft to put on my white linen suit. The effect, that of a good bracing shower, put me in a mood for celebration, for now we had escaped and now nothing stood in our way, and we could continue downstream in the new country, perhaps to live, to settle in the warm exile of the glow of each other's eyes, locked in an embrace that would never quite fit, yet an embrace which could offer a lifetime of promise.

Yet it was all over. Damn her eyes!

*There they stood.* His treachery, already written on his face, now rolled out upon his tongue. He told me was *sorry* (!) but he had decided to go back to the capital with the woman. But he was not really sorry. I could see that. I could see everything, and now I only wanted one thing, to be alone—and quickly.

Mentally I fired him. So that I might watch, not my servant, but my ex-servant step aboard the speedboat with the Païnted Wōman, watch the water churn, hear it gurgle, hear a death rattle, be alone.

Yet can I be certain? Can I really be certain that it was not I who abandoned my servant or ex-servant for her?

Can I ever know this?

✦

I am writing this on the raft.

After they left I was so exhausted from recent events (whatever they are!) that I bypassed a state of depression to fall straight into a deep and nightmared sleep, which I hesitate to call my own: I would call it another's sleep. I was, perhaps, nightmared. By the sun, the sun's glare, who was dreaming daylight.

Or something like that.

But this sleep must have lasted a full twenty-four hours. There is no other way to account for the stopped watch. The position of the raft, the oddly familiar angle of the sun. I awoke to discover my self lying flat on my back, left arm thrown above my head, fingers hanging limp in warm water and being nibbled at by a small green fish.

I sat up. In the very middle of the ocean. Sleep I wanted then, any sleep, anyone's, away from this, for on a twisting neck at every degree of the compass there was only a thin, slightly hazy line of horizon, a situation utterly unique in my travels. The raft lay silent under me; it bore no marks of a violent splash which might account for this watered desolation, and the log-thongs were tight, the baggage intact. But the sea was odd, definitely odd, and I am hard-pressed to describe its condition then, which was waveless, windless and of a surface as flat as glass, matte rather than glossy, and of a water clouded with a fine golden silt which was or at least tasted fresh, as of the most hidden and inaccessible mountain springs.

So I would not die of thirst. I reasoned that we were being slowly carried farther out to sea one way or another and that there was little to be done about it; and I had things to do. I took off my white linen suit, now brushed my teeth, shaved, combed my hair in the perfect reflection of the calm waters, now went and urinated off one side of the raft where, owing to an unsteadiness brought on by too much staying in bed of late, I lost my balance and fell face-first into the water. I expected, in that flash of falling, an interminable plunge. But no, never.

The water was only three feet deep. As one will discover land in the most unexpected places. The bottom, soft and smooth, almost as uniformly flat as the surface of the water, was interrupted only by a few large stones imbedded in the sand, and this over as large an area as I had the energy to explore by foot. I used one of these stones to anchor the raft pending, I suppose, further developments.

The little green fish was the only fish I ever saw, and there were no birds, no clouds, no seaweed, no drifting objects, and sometimes it seemed that even the raft was not, nor my seeing this nothingness, nor I.

This was the center of an indescribable, and time stopped. The sun appeared motionless, yet was not too hot, and I rolled off the raft into the water, again and again, for sport and entertainment. What else was there to do? Whenever hungry, I ate from the array of river fish laid out to dry on the luggage. In the conventional sense, days and days passed—elsewhere, not here, but that much time, yes, and I searched for everything on this blank sea, in this blank sky, in the rough texture of the logs—my bed, my house, my grave—but saw no more than the development of one minor, boring phenomenon, that of waves, of little waves made by my moving about on the raft, my swimming and pacing back and forth, little waves that expanded, ballooned away from the raft until they vanished over the horizons some forty-five minutes later, never to return, for no waves ever came back from those horizons, nor even the slightest ripple.

As you will hear no breath besides your own.

One day, so to speak, I collected all the stones I could find underwater and piled them in one place, then dug under the sand or mud for more and was happy to find an almost unlimited supply. I now anchored the other end of the raft, thus creating a straight edge to sight down, an axis which cut through my as yet small pile of rocks and through, ten feet beyond, the point at which I would dig out more rocks. In this manner I excluded the possibility of getting lost underwater and undoing my own work, which was to be a tower. First I laid out a circle of rocks about seven feet in diameter, now proceeded to dump rocks inside it until, after much work, the tower broke the surface of the water. Now I had to change the place of my rock supply, for the hole in the bottom was as deep as the tower was tall. Of course there are purists who will argue that the one was no more of an achievement than the other; however, I point out that it was within the realm of possibility to construct the tower from stones gathered from the surface, though grossly more inefficient than digging a hole.

From another source I added more stones towards an ideal height of five feet, seven inches above the surface of the water, and for the final layers I first put the stones on the raft, then climbed on it myself, and from there reached over to the tower. Into the segment facing the raft I fitted stones in such a way as to form a series of steps; otherwise, in scaling the side of the tower to the platform at the top, I would risk dislodging a stone and weakening the structure, to which I was becoming attached. Everything held nicely under my weight, but from the top of the tower I could see no more than from the raft or the water. Indeed, I had expected as much, and only from idleness did I now elevate myself to tiptoes where, surprisingly, I thought to detect a thin black line where the sky lay upon the darker horizon of sea like a wall under indirect lighting, a thin black line which might have been something else.

Yet I was not up high enough to be certain whether it was land or illusion, so I jumped towards the water in search of more rocks. In mid-air it occurred to me that I could have used one of the suitcases—the thought blanked out a moment of sensation—perhaps I was splashing around underwater—but at some instant, sudden and seeming precise, the sun plunged into the sea and there came a darkness, almost total, almost as black as within a tightly shut closet, within, even, the chamber of an idle camera.

I stood up in the water. In the light of a few dim stars I now eyed a nearby black form.

It was only the raft. I went to it. The crystalline stones of the tower emitted the softest of white glows.

And now the waves came back. Slowly at first, gently but growing sharper and higher, from which side I could not tell. But only one side, not all around. Suddenly there was a gurgle nearby, and now the dim white disk of the top of the tower vanished into the black waters. So man's works are engulfed, even those meant to pass the time. A wave struck, dropped upon me as I was scrambling to secure myself in the center of the raft and tore away one of the heiress's remaining pieces of luggage, which bobbed away on another course, no longer mine, trailing from its cracks billows upon billows of a phosphorescent red and illuminating my part of the sea in crimson waves and bright bubbles.

Until it sank, and a screaming hurricane rose to cover all the sea, to carry off all her luggage, and I lay down tired from my recent, fruitless exertions, determined to sleep through this one.

✢

The hurricane has left, and I am here, resting up in a not uncomfortable room in this tropical city's best hotel, that is, the only one which was not blown down in the storm. I've been using the terrace, which has a nice view of the water, to dry my white linen suit, the only thing that got wet. There is virtually nothing to see in these overgrown parts, I am led to believe, so will move on as soon as I am recuperated.

From nothing in particular, mind you.

✦

A waiter bringing me a drink in a bar this afternoon collapsed at my feet with an awful clatter of tray and broken glass. I stood up in alarm, but the proprietor motioned me to sit down. It would seem that the waiter, who soon was snoring, just went to sleep. That was the event of the day. I never got my drink. These are a race of amber-haired, green-eyed men whose expressions of somnolent dissipation suggest that they have sunk irretrievably into the depths of vice. Owing to a great number of very artfully done manikins, it is impossible to estimate the population of this town—even if you could find the energy to start counting. There are, for example, some twenty of these sitting on benches in a small public park facing the port. Exactly what purpose they serve (and in fact they occupy the best places) I fail to understand, nor can I expect to be told: the hotel staff, who speak a sort of English on occasion, answer all questions with a glazed smile, followed by a yawn. I came back to find a languid chambermaid stretched out naked on my bed (and now is virtually at my side), and though young and attractive, her presence is hindering my work. Something will have to be done. These are dark-haired (indeed, the hair is black), blue-eyed women who seem to be almost of a different race than the men. And she snores.

✦

I imagine this sort of thing will happen now and then.

Along the waterfront there is an esplanade facing out to sea and shaded by tall, spindly trees somewhat like palms, and a row of benches where lounge a few of these manikins. Curiosity aroused, I went down there this morning and sat next to one of them. They are odd things, made out of cast iron and painted or whitewashed over in a careful but eccentric manner—features, clothes, etc., although the shoes are real, albeit without laces (stolen?). In their old-fashioned way they seem to be better dressed than the townspeople, who will pay no attention at all to them. I gather they are placed only outdoors.

With nothing else to do I intended to spend most of the day there, alternately enjoying the view of the sea and examining the manikins. There are some little puzzles that seem worth getting to the bottom of. For example, was anything *inside* the casting? (Money?) And I kept an eye on the rest of the town. After a time the city's unique bus, a flatbed truck fitted with benches, rumbled by as it does once a day, lurching across the innumerable potholes to be found all over the city, and now, this time, I noticed what I had not previously: that all passengers were manikins. Frankly this was an interesting discovery, and thus absorbed in its meaning I failed to pay much attention to a snapping sound far above my head until, a few seconds later, an enormous fruit (what is found on the ground is a vegetable, what comes from the sky is a fruit), an enormous fruit, as large as a watermelon but with hair twice as long as a coconut's, dropped to the ground only inches away. The force of the impact flung me over the backside of the bench. I left the esplanade in great haste, brushing sand out of my hair as I went.

✢

Now I realize: there exists no transportation either in or out of this city. My raft, confiscated by customs, lies anchored in the small port, the only craft there, and now and then a townsperson stops on the quay to stare at it, soon falls to sleep on the spot. This place suffers from a singular lack of presence of mind. But not I. I made a foot tour of the outer ring of town. We are completely surrounded by impenetrable jungle. The railroad tracks end at the trunk of a giant fern-like tree whose growth has bent the rails straight up in the air. Armed with this discovery and more, and I was angry, I came back to the hotel and beat the manager to within an inch of his life, to make him confess how I could leave. I have had quite enough of his stinking yawns! Through sheer laziness and lack of willpower he has become a semi-invalid who will move only between his bed (which is in his office) and his desk. There had to be a way out. After all, the town, though primitive, has such amenities as (fluctuating) electricity, canned goods, one 'modern' hotel, etc., and all these objects were brought in here some way.

Blood flowed before he decided to explain. Or demonstrate. His desk was littered with old cigarette wrappers, bills, scraps of paper, coconut hair, and now towards these he dropped his head, puffed up his cheeks and blew them away. By which he meant, I understood only after having resumed the beating, hurricanes.

But I will not wait on the roof, suitcase in hand, for the next one to come along. Not without a reserved seat.

And I had a conference with the chambermaid, who has left for the next room. Or I have. The rooms are identical and it is hard to tell. This humid heat can make one very tired. However she was of no help whatsoever with these questions and wanted to ramble on about other things, sadly irrelevant to my plight.

But I can rest now that she has left and has taken away her nakedness, which trailed after her, glaring like an indescribable shadow.

---

Perhaps it was a mistake to have ventured forth once again into this silly town, but I did, for there was nothing else to do but walk around, and so walk around I did—to discover a cast iron manikin of *myself* sitting on a bench. Fair enough! It would enhance tourism. So I thought. Of course, I should add that it was exactly identical to all the other castings I have seen. Which observation raised in me an overwhelming sense of frustration. But I went on. The wooden buildings were falling apart for the incredibly simple reason that the nails were never driven all the way in. Whole sides of houses are open and exposed. The things that went on! These are a people who care nothing for privacy. I walked on, reaching the central square which I had not visited before, and admired its typical landmark, a stone clock tower. However, inside a basket suspended from the clock face sat a small boy, some fifteen feet above the ground where stood a cardboard carton with a few greenish coins inside. I waited there five minutes by my reliable watch. The hands of the clock did not move, nor did the boy, who amused himself by staring down at me. I don't know what adventurous spirit possessed me then, but I pulled out my wallet and dropped into the carton a banknote of the local equivalent of around two dollars. The boy smiled sweetly, stood up in his basket, moved the hands of the clock around from 2:10 to 8:47.

Ha! That was that. Now I resumed my walk.

Suddenly the great coconut-like fruit started raining down everywhere, each striking the pavement with an incredible bang, sending up chips of concrete, pebbles, clouds of dust, or crashing through the wooden buildings, which promptly began to collapse. I noticed with some horror that they were the only type of tree in town. Taking to my heels in a zigzag course, I ran back towards the hotel. Why I was not annihilated by a falling fruit I do not know to this day. Nor was that all. As soon as the fruit struck the ground they sprouted open and started growing with a rapidity which was not to be believed, and this, I knew, was the visibly growing forest, about which I have heard a great deal.

The bombardment was still going on when I reached the hotel, now completely deserted, and the streets were clogging up with a forest almost five feet high in places, already impenetrable in others. I raced up to my room. Most of the coconut-like fruit had bounced off the solid roof, but the roots of those that had not were already thrusting their way through the ceiling, fat grey roots. I stepped out on the terrace a moment, sheltered by an overhang from the bombardment, which seemed to be diminishing. From there I could survey what was left of the town: a growing forest. The small harbor was of course gone. And I watched the trees thrust still higher, I watched their clogged treetops raise towards the sky my raft, the city's unique bus, a park bench with manikins. All birds had been scared off. And now the town sank into silence as the bombardment ceased altogether, and the only sound to be heard was the soft rustling of leaves as they unfolded and now and then slapped together in weird applause; higher and higher the trees soared, passing the fifth floor, towards annexing the whole sky, blocking it down to a small blue square directly above the hotel, a distant skylight, until the moment when—as my heart stopped—the fronds thickened, slowly knit together, to plunge the world below into a slimy green glow of darkness.

Then the bombardment resumed.

Lighting matches one after another on the run, I threw myself down five flights of stairs through a rain of falling plaster and a traffic of furiously growing grey roots to reach the end and shelter, the basement door. Which I slammed and latched behind me. All was now quiet. The basement room somewhat resembled the one I had just given up on the top floor, or rather, both rooms up there, but why anyone should have installed a fully furnished room here, underground, is beyond imagining. I now inspected the room. Clearly someone had been living here recently. On the nightstand next to the bed, which was hard and narrow, lay a stack of current magazines in the strange tongues of all the neighboring regions, and under them—my curiosity aroused by a bulge—a sort of album filled with scraps of paper and bits of photographs, hard to make any sense of. And I didn't bother. But I was led on by this discovery to the opposite side of the room, to a small table, yet large enough to write on and the proper height for that, whose single drawer was locked. Now this was interesting. The lock seemed to be of a very common sort, and on the chance that one of my keys might fit, and I do actually possess a desk very similar to this one, I tried them all out and was delighted to feel the lock respond.

Inside the drawer was an unloaded .22 pistol. And a box of cartridges. Rare is it that one finds a room not only well furnished in this world, but equipped as well with a means of defense. Immediately I felt less worried about the jungle growing outside the door. For now I was prepared.

I should say that the electricity, oddly enough, was still functioning down here, and the room was bathed in an even, pure light from a solitary fixture in the exact center of the ceiling, and owing to a handsome wallpaper patterned in dabs of blue and violet, one would have imagined, or like to have imagined, that one was deep under the sea, not the ground. But that is neither here nor there. Everything seemed in order, so I made myself at home, that is, stripped off all my clothes and climbed into bed. Where I am now, resting up from recent events.

That is, where I have been for some time.

Yet, glad as I was to escape the last cataclysm of a world outside, and having soon made as detailed a description of it as I could bear, there appeared to be nothing left for me to do. I could see, with a startling clarity, boredom coming.

I got out of bed and paced back and forth in my bare feet across the soft blue carpet. A pleasant sensation to the bottoms of the feet. And the unaccustomed swinging motion of the body. Yet tiring, very tiring, so I went back to the bed. This bed was an interesting object. (Perhaps all beds are.) And I cannot praise the variety of textures too highly: the sheets, which were smooth, almost glossy and of a whiteness so radiant as to make one gasp at the catching of it square in the eye. A fulsome pillow, an electric blanket of a fuzzy blue material, which some misguided enthusiast for modernity had ordered imported into this jungle, against perhaps the expectation of another ice age, like tomorrow; but returning to the bed from my pacing back and forth, I could not but admire the interesting way in which all these things, sheets, pillows, blanket, were all crumpled together.

And thus I was led to examine the structure of the bed; I knelt, lifted up the mattress and looked at the engineering. Nor was there anyone under the bed, thank God! The bed frame consisted of an agreeable intermingling of wood and metal, and I made a mental picture of it, so as to have some notion, a clear image, of the structure which supported me when I next lay down, which I soon did.

I mention this as physical antecedent. An act. That is all. For I cannot account for what happened all of a sudden—such is the nature of the world's smallest electrical charge—but there are thoughts, a multitude of thoughts swarming at a precipice, which I could not express. Or: would not express. Not with pen and paper. Not with the jarring collision of a pen-point against the deserted plain of a blank sheet of paper, beneath the unseen amphitheatre of thousands of eyes, or that single pair which might be in a next room; and whom, the so-called readers, I lead on the forced march of tourism for no reason at all, to be honest, except that we all like to travel. Or something like that. Some will say that there comes, inevitably, a parting of the ways. But I will say: no, there never comes a parting of the ways, and that is the problem.

They, those eyes, you, are always there so long as the possibility exists of seeing what there is to be seen. And if there is paper, it will be seen, and what is written on it.

So I took away the paper. And everything like paper. So that they, those eyes, you, could no longer watch (or hold the potentiality of watching), so that I might be truly alone and free, to give my thoughts a sublimely private birth, with a ballpoint pen, upon the skin of my very own body.

Which I must now describe.

My leg-hair being of a particularly fine variety, I found no obstacle to beginning my composition at the left knee and working up the thigh to the crotch; then over to the right knee, and down. I preferred to use my feet for notes and comments. Smoothest writing of all was across the loins, proceeding upwards to that point of the chest where the hand cramped to a halt; and as I am neither athletic nor agile and wished to study my work in a comfortable position, reclining naturally in bed, I left the backsides quite blank; and saved a very special place for the title, or the thought of ultimate intimacy.

I call this activity *somatography*. For whatever it's worth.

And I should think that in writing on the face of the sun a writing which cannot be seen through the glare, and thus which remains intact, whole, untouched, because not seen, that one might also write upon the sheets of a bed, the bedclothes, upon carpets, walls, buildings and cities, writing which would remain concealed in precise proportion to the degree with which the surface—that sheet or carpet—asserted its own texture, its own character. And upon, perhaps, the bodies of others.

So one might inscribe the world. Which could not otherwise be described.

When finished, and with nothing else to do, I got out of bed and found a door which led to a short hallway; at its end, there was a modern bathroom where I shaved and brushed my teeth and combed my hair. My smile, as seen in the mirror, was of a special freshness this evening and somehow supplied me with the extra energy required for the next move. Which was to return to the room and dress, then step outside for a breath of badly needed fresh air.

## II. After a Fashion

⁕

As a rule I travel only in underdeveloped countries but here and there I come to a progress-blighted land and the only thing to do is cross it as fast as I can, and be done with it. I am now in a first-class compartment of a rapid express train winding its way through a deep snow-filled canyon; it is dawn—as much as there will ever be one with these clouds—and the window is a bright blue screen of dim winter light, now drained of color—or not yet filled with color—beyond that tinge, and framed with little parabolas of frost in the corners of the glass. The compartment is empty again, though there still hangs over it the odor of a cigar, an opened purse, a string bag of sweating oranges, and I have been able to catch up on my notes; and as the train rolls and slides and bangs over the rails, my pen, skittering across these pages, makes a weak mimic of those sounds—but the train will always go faster than I write.

We are passing through a region of agriculture and woodcutting: dairy cattle, timber mills, small peaked houses bearing a yard of snow, a rare inhabitant outside, bundled up and walking down traces of a snowed-over road, his head leaking steam from mouth, eyes, ears; or as we speed past to the clang of bells, a car waiting at a crossing and festooned with mists, snow and, drooping behind the tires, frosty turds. What business they have outside in cold like this must be all their own. Or, after all, they might only be coming to catch one of these cylinders of heated air that slash across their frozen subaqueous countryside ten times a day.

Of the passengers in the train, and there are few, most seem to be local travelers on the way to work in that always the next town; dressed in heavy overcoats, they sit straight in their seats, polished briefcase to one side, newspaper in hand, and stare at the glass, but never through it. Others like myself, but not identical, others who are here for a longer term, a day or two or three, who occupy their compartments with a disorder of luggage, of food packages, books, of posture, of thought, in order to mask the veneer walls, soften the intractable angle of seats, to outwit, or try, the pane of vision—the window that permits us a view of where we are now, but not where we have been, or will be, except on the sharpest of bends—and these passengers are the ones who haunt the passageways, platforms, restrooms, and pace up and down the moving length of the train as if to compound the irreversible thrust forward with thousands of tiny epicycles, in search of precious instants of reversal. They are a sad lot: twitching, wincing, contracting themselves in the fear that their filth will seep through their clothes and become visible, calibrating station house and mountain and valley against notions of halfway there, almost there, there in a minute or two, *there, here* in the arms of a destination; and their irritation and boredom is the real power behind this expensive train as it rushes across a wasteland of being nowhere at all, a public noisome moment in the hermetical privacy of a life. And when they get off, we give a sigh of relief, the brakes discharge their load of steam, and we move on, that much more alone, towards a destination that seems pleasantly far away, one that cannot be compared.

✧

When I first caught the train I was, as now, alone in the compartment which I had taken for lack of anything better. After washing and shaving in the restroom a few steps down the corridor, I intended to get some much-needed sleep and was about to stretch out on the hard and narrow bench, having first folded up the armrests, when smoke began to pour out from underneath. 'For God's sake, is this going to start all over again?' I muttered, pulling down the window. Now, of all things, the smoke stopped. Why, I could not say. The machinery found under train seats is usually incredible. That it stopped (or started) was my concern. Once the compartment was properly aired, I pushed the window closed and lay down again, laid my head to vibrate against the glass, and fell to sleep to the blurred rise and fall of telegraph poles and the roll of endless fields of wheat.

Some hours later, with the train still moving (it might have stopped in my sleep), the compartment door rumbled open. Instinctively I retracted my legs a few inches, adrift between wakefulness and dreamfully pretending that I was welcoming more passengers into the compartment. A great fuss in lifting some luggage to the rack finally roused me to sit up. I now had as fellow travelers an attractive young woman, a portly gentleman with a cigar, and a tall, emaciated fellow carrying a string bag of oranges and a book—he might have been a priest. Something about both of these men was odd, was not quite there, or where it should have been. Perhaps for his seeming age, the portly gentleman's hairline was much too low, as if he might be wearing a hairpiece; and he seemed not to know what to do with his cigar, which hand to hold it in, or how to grasp it firmly in his mouth, and though portly, he carried his weight with ease, as if perhaps it was only a very artful job of padding. And the same for the priestly fellow: his glasses seemed to be decorative, not functional, for behind them there was no distortion of his green eyes, but I could not tell what made him look thinner than he actually was, or whether it was make-up that gave his face such a funereal air. Nor could I be sure the two were wearing disguises; it seemed so, and it seemed also that under them the two men were probably very much alike in appearance, perhaps even brothers.

There was an extraordinary bicycle parked in the corridor outside, and passersby kept hooking their cuffs and pockets on it as they squeezed past.

The priestly fellow sat down next to me and opened his book and looked down at it, but to what end I am not sure for I never saw him turn a page. The young woman sat opposite me, and now, wide awake, I recognized her. She is the one whom at times and at times not I have called the Païnted Wōman, meaning of course a woman who looks like a painting—is attractive—neither more nor less. I believe she recognized me. Of no importance—our confrontation promised to last only the duration of this particular stage of my voyage (and, coincidentally hers, at this moment) and I was neither troubled nor pleased. We sat in silence for a long time, lulled by the railroad noises I have described elsewhere until finally I was moved to make a few remarks out of politeness. She listened intently, kindly did not interrupt me. My words:

'If I am not mistaken, it seems that the curious forces that may or may not govern this world have willed this coming together, this tumultuous rushing down the tracks towards the next station where you but probably not I will get off, and since it is thus, we should stand aside a ways and attempt to look at this moment in its proper perspective. I am going to go to great lengths to do this, which I hope you will appreciate. Though it may well be that this is impossible, that there is no accident, that you have tracked me down here to have the last word, or the first. If I talk in extremes, madam, it is to save time. We live by means and compromises, and of this I do not often wish to be reminded, and you, in your presence here, remind me of that, and so I turn to a very practical matter in spite of myself, with all the difficulties it entails. Where to start? God only knows, yet I alone must choose. But to begin. Oddly, the only time I can ask you for my freedom is when you are here and I have, by definition, lost it, as I lose it now, during this our briefly joint train ride. But in what manner, you may ask with some impatience, am I now enslaved?

'That is a good question. Can I even answer it? Perhaps I could only begin to answer it by asking you a question, something like: would you feel at home, comfortable, at rest, adequately entertained, contented *as part of* and surrounded by nothing but a mathematical equation? Imagine, if you will, you sitting there as you are now, your heart beating away, tears ready to spring to your eyes, your arms trembling towards an embrace, but surrounded by numbers and letters and signs and *nothing else*. Would you ever sit quietly as part of that, and of your own choice? You will think not, and I will agree. Yet, while you sit there, near me, I am enslavable, and I must climb down from the equation (where I would be at rest) and ask you something as simple as how you are, or climb down just to look, because I heard a noise—and there are no noises within that equation—and then you will ask me what I am doing up there (and you can ask so many things without even opening your lips) and I will explain, as I have many times before, and you will say something about a fresh peach pie which I will then smell, and so on, on and on, until by an act of what you would call cruelty,

I must tear myself away from you, cursing and weeping, to return to that invention which I cannot stand but cannot do without and leave what you would call this earth—and it is that, and it is where you belong, but not I, the point from where you will tell me that I should not stay up there so long. But in forever, there is, my dear, no length.

'So I ask of you one thing. That you not seek me out, wherever I may be, and no matter how much I may seek you, to whatever lengths I may go, you must repulse me, throw me back. To where? I don't know. Perhaps to where I am going. But if you refuse, I must freeze you in a paralysis of presence without person, a number in a series, and there is only one way I can do this that I know of. Or perhaps two. Neither of which can I speak.'

But she would not agree to my demand.

'You must!'

A whistle screamed and the train roared across a trestle over a very fetching gully.

She spoke now at more length, but with a dangerous hysteria, all the time fidgeting with her dark lavender skirt. Turning over the hem and turning it back, exposing and recovering an inch more of shapely knee, upon which the eyes of our two fellow travelers bent in frequent glance. When she had finished speaking, I thought that now, at last, we would pass into the silence from which we emerged.

But I was wrong.

For the man disguised as a portly gentleman cleared his throat and said in a loud, ringing voice: 'My dear newfound friends, I beg you an infinite pardon, but I could not help but overhear you from my reserved seat in this modestly furnished first-class compartment. And so having unavoidably overheard you, I cannot refrain from making a comment or two upon the remarkable situation that has developed, and of which I and the book-reading young man, and I see it is *my* book he is reading, have become unwitting witnesses. What he says, however, is his own business, not mine, and if he so wishes it is all right with me if he has his crack at the situation too. But first permit me to present my credentials. I am a certified public connubial therapist with a veterinary degree. My bachelor's thesis dealing with the pleasure problem in artificial insemination won a big prize. I was the one who achieved fructuous wedlock between an unhappy pair of all but extinct and thus rarest of all bears. My privately printed treatise on sexual engineering is held in respect by the reputable and disreputable alike. But I need not overwhelm you with more. Now you, my newfound friend in the white linen suit, made a most apt allusion to the perspective one has from distance, a distance which I, as outsider and accidental witness, do indeed have. I do not know either of you, have never seen you before and will positively never see you again. You may even have noticed that I am traveling incognito and thus even if you do see me again, you will not recognize me. Within this speeding train therefore, I am distance, I am perspective, in relation to you sitting there, thus you should have some interest in my opinion of the matter you are discussing. I am unbiased, objective, without the slightest taint of prejudice. What I say in relation to you, and considering my credentials, must be the absolute truth. You may accuse me of taking sides, but no, it is hardly that. The sides are *there* without being chosen. I—'

He faltered at the peculiar intensity of my stare and, lest he resume, I added quietly that he was either wrong or didn't know what he was talking about, most likely both; and as he closed his mouth, which had been left open, there came from it a little clinking noise, of teeth colliding with teeth, and I knew that thereafter he would be silent. I now directed my gaze to the priestly young man, who promptly broke into sweat while ever so slowly moving forward the book he was not reading, to cover an unmistakable erectile bulge in his lap.

Thus we rode in silence to the next stop where all three of them got off. I kissed the young lady goodbye, more from habit than anything. I am not sure whether I was glad to be alone again—and in a way I was not, for this last reunion hung over me like a great untidiness. In spite of appearances, the last word remained and will always remain unutterable.

⚜

The conductor informs me that we will presently be in New Curio City, the country's second largest city and principal manufacturing center. I will have to wait over there a day and a half in order to catch the next train out. Last time I was through, it was only a matter of four hours, a not unreasonable wait. There is a special quality about New Curío City, in that from a distance one always anticipates seeing it again; yet, as one approaches and the distance dissolves, this anticipation sours into reluctance, finally into abhorrence. In that sense, I am almost there.

And indeed, here, rushing past, are the first of the far-flung suburbs of New Curío City. Tall narrow houses on muddy plots of ground, strangled by iron debris, wires, pipes which have been dropped here on this outer edge to rust and crumble. Smoking mills. Eternally peripheral highways. A shiny vehicle speeding, as far as I or anyone else on this train can see, to nowhere. I comb my memory but find I know not one soul in this city. I will stay in a hotel, I will hold my nose until the next train leaves. The brakes have been applied; heavily we are slowing down, grinding out showers of sparks and clouds of steel dust ...

✧

This air transfixes. The window is open. The city mutters through the room upon a breeze from a sky of hazy brown air which almost blots out the distant range of mountains, yet a breeze that is only scented of the city, not clogged, as it flows past me to rustle the papers on this twenty-times-waxed table. I have been sitting here all morning watching a parallelogram of sunlight creep across the carpet towards my foot, fabricating laments for all time that I have known, conversing with each fragrance as it drifts in the window, a single strand of cobweb, and around the room to be sucked out, so suddenly, through the crack under the door. No, it is not a day for moving around, it is a day which of itself unfolds, a flower—to be cut.

✧

Through a series of little coincidental gestures this morning while checking in, going up to my room, sending out my extra suit to be pressed and so on, my attention became directed, indeed concentrated upon a fellow guest who must have arrived here about the same time, also a foreigner, perhaps the same age as I. Seemingly preoccupied by some grave matter, He noticed nothing around Him, nothing beyond His immediate reach, much less my gaze which became all the more steady for being ignored. Had He once looked up to stare at me, surely I would have looked away and dropped the matter. What's the matter? Nothing's the matter. I mean: I would have resumed ignoring Him, not seeing Him.

That evening I was in the lobby pretending to inspect pictures in magazines, pictures of people who speak in captions but will not be spoken to, when He came down the stairs and stood before the main door as if trying to make up His mind to go out. With only a few feet between us, virtually within reach of one another, I made my presence apparent by rattling the magazine pages, coughing, swearing, casting ambiguous phrases at the ceiling and repeatedly looking up at Him. He took no notice. And went out. And this was the invitation that could not be refused, for clearly I was being invited to be involved, or to witness, or to know. To know what He would reveal. My palms were pressed upon the glass door before it had even stopped swinging. Yes, there He was on the sidewalk, waiting to hear my footsteps behind Him.

In the warm night a traffic of breezes circulated through the city in sweet-smelling puffs, down long wide boulevards of light which were like illuminated bridges across an unseen gulf, forgotten; and down miles of sticky sidewalks I followed Him, on a crooked line, an insinuation and in keeping a proper distance behind, engrossed in my subtle geometry, I failed to notice for some time that His walk was disordered and without real destination: He was wandering. Now towards a bright sign (with a smiling face), towards an illuminated building, now a cardboard crowd on a corner. Now He would stop, turn, cross a boulevard and go back down the other side, now He would pause to peer over the silhouettes of window shoppers into a glowing frame. He seemed not to care where He was going or had come from, and soon I sensed that I knew more than He and that He would have to turn around, and might, to find out where He was. For directions. The possibility amused me. I would give them, now continue to follow Him. But He wandered on, the world's longest stroll, while I searched the surfaces of the many mirrors that the prosperous, clothes-hidden citizens of New Curío City have laid against the walls, I searched in them an image of His probably absent face but saw only my anxious pursuit in transit, a little more rapid than a fuzzy blur like a crowd.

Where was He going?—I must have asked myself many times. Who was He looking for?

A woman? But if so, He found none, not that night, not along the boulevards which radiated to a distant glowing horizon, not in the façades of the central square, not in the black clouds of shrubbery which hovered over the very middle of the square above a subterranean toilet, where old men gravitated around bare light-bulbs in search of the best of all available urinals—not in a cafe whose delta of tangled chairs flowed across the sidewalk, having sprung from a deep red cavern of glittering glass and jewelry—yet here He paused longer than usual, facing the central square. It was a sign, a sign which I could read, and so I squeezed through a snarl of chair legs to a table towards the back and sat down. Yes. Now He half turned towards me, yet turned not more than a fragment of an eye, and took a table up front, now faced away from me again, towards the central square. It was a welcome rest. My feet were swollen by the warmth, my palms creased with sweat. He drank coffee and watched passersby. Perhaps He was waiting for someone, or anyone, perhaps myself, and I might even have gone up and introduced myself—that I had seen Him at the hotel, how did He like New Curío City? But why should I do that? No, there was no sense in complicating His wait for this woman in this really excellent cafe for waiting, the brightest of all places we have passed, at a floodlit corner, at a confluence of odors from a dozen carry-away food stands, with a fine view of a great electric sign on a building opposite, featuring an orange neon man, walking furiously, stiffly, advertising God knows what.

Concerning this woman, for whom I discovered, with a shock, I was now in wait, I indulged in a number of precise notions in order to pass, perhaps, that time, such as her familiar walk which He was now trying to make out in the otherwise mechanical crowd, and I even posited for Him an hour at which she was to arrive, a quarter past something, a human, reasonable quarter of an hour past the end of an event in another part of town, an end which was a beginning of the rendezvous to be consummated fifteen minutes later. (She never showed up!) I was wrong, very probably bored. He continued scanning passersby, staining each one of them with the negative of unrecognition. Or something had gone wrong, something whose seriousness was calibrated by the moving hands of a watch—she would be held up in traffic—an accident would prevent her—she had willfully refused to come this evening—which? Every meeting is a reconciliation. For whom? For some. Perhaps—and I may not be doing Him justice—He did not even set a rendezvous—perhaps she had no idea He was here—perhaps at one time this had been their habitual place of meeting at this same hour, in the past (which is always distant) and He had come here this evening, the first time in years, to break through a time-dried crust, had come here only to discover that He could not do it alone without her, that she had to come here as instinctively as He had, at this habitual hour, for now the only way to smash down those intervening years was through a miracle of coincidence, a something almost outside either of their infected selves, a something to prime, pump and refresh their desires. And even had I been certain He possessed it, this expectation, I would not have rushed over to point out the fallacy of His wait, the fallacy which was, after all, that their rendezvous of some years ago, the trappings and aura of which He now desired to resuscitate, had not they led to this moment of utter desperation. And thus, would this not happen again? And again? And again? For there was a less than total certainty in a probably two-fold failure—that she would not arrive, that if she did arrive no course would be changed— and that is why I let Him wait in a hardening metal chair at a bright yellow table, with a ring of cold coffee in the bottom of a cup, for another fifteen minutes, and still another, until a whole hour had passed, until I assumed He had accepted His irreversible solitude—as it would be—while yet guarding within Himself a closed spring of joy that would gush forth at her now impossible arrival.

It was beyond midnight now and night-plumaged crowds were leaving the cafes for taxis, buses and radial boulevards; it was time to go, and when He stood up I sensed in the air, extending from Him to me, a network as of the finest of wires, which had been limp, now go taut and lift me to my feet and put me to walking behind, that set distance, but now strung up, tied, geared, enmeshed, gesture of body to body of gesture; or perhaps we suffered a similar fatigue of muscles, which made all movement seem heavy and fettered. The crowds were soon gone, but to little difference, for their pictures still lay against the walls, brighter and more distinct than they had ever been, and I lengthened the distance between us, now slipped to another side of a boulevard to cut footsteps and breathings too twinned for this silence of now: I would not want to hamper Him.

And in fact He soon paused and retraced His steps to a window display. I walked on towards the point opposite, a telephone pole, where, head excepted, I faded. Back to me and facing the window He now studied—either what was behind the glass or what was reflected in it, the latter being perhaps Himself, the street behind Him, the phone pole, my head. To this day I do not know. I know only what I could see. He pulled a pipe from His coat pocket and placed it in His mouth without lighting it. The window display, at which He might have been looking, was of a dining room. A long mahogany table. Perhaps a dozen chairs with high backs, of a style neither medieval nor modern. Three thin white candles. And enclosing the display were stage walls of white, hung with a good number of paintings—far too many in fact, for they attracted attention away from the expensive dining room set, put there, after all, to be looked at and sold. (Yes: a furniture store.) Only one could I make out at all clearly from my distance, a large painting of a nude woman reclining on a bed of blue, of water or of flowers, set directly behind the table. It might have seemed that the owner of the store was something of a collector, wished to show his paintings in public—but to the confusion of his interests as merchant and as collector. You see the result: He had stopped to look at the paintings—good or not, I had no idea from my distance—and not at the furniture, and of this I was now certain. (Before leaving New Curío City I had intended to go back to that store and look at the paintings from a better angle, in order to acquire certain speculative notions of the character of the one I was following—and, for that matter, of the merchant himself. But time fell short.)

He studied the paintings for close to a half-hour.

We wandered through the night, in a circle, back to the central square, now deserted, now only half-illuminated, where now the neon man, walking up an orange sweat, reigned supreme, advertising God knows what to, say, a full moon. He climbed in a taxi. I let Him drive off before catching a second one. It must have seemed odd that He should want to drive back to the hotel when it was only a few blocks away. But I was wrong. Taxi behind taxi we drove up and down those very same boulevards I had blistered my feet on, rolled on with a giddy ease, now far into the suburbs where lamps held the places of sleeping owners or an absent sun, crisscrossing the town back and forth, while the meter ticked up comical totals—comical, yes, for were we ever to meet in the future, in another place, I am sure we would talk over the whole episode and laugh and laugh at the time and expense one of us went to to follow the other who in fact was only wandering through the city to wear away a boredom, a desperation with a fatiguing variety of sensations, and I told all this to the taxi driver, I imagined Him telling something very like it to His driver—yet I was wrong. In a residential area perhaps not far from the center of town, He stepped from the taxi and sent it away. (To spare Him I dropped my head below the window and got out fifty feet beyond.) He was standing in a clump of bushes at the edge of a lawn. The house was an impressive single-storey dwelling composed of a variety of wings. He appeared to be loading a pistol. The house was of a modern, block-like style, with few windows facing the street. But there was one, and He vanished into it. By now it was easily dawn and I perceived that with His disappearance my pursuit was at an end, and before turning away in search of another taxi I silently wished Him Godspeed in whatever He had to do.

Then, walking away under the earliest and deepest of blue morning skies, I understood: He had wanted someone with Him up until the very edge of the irreversible moment. There was nothing else I could have done.

※

Somewhere, in another part of the world, very far distant from where I am, some small event of troubling significance has just taken place. I am sitting up in my late morning bed, aroused by that instant of intimacy, sharp and explosive, that has pierced the very center of my being. I suppose that is what was meant by the 'shot heard round the world'. I have heard something, at any rate.

✦

But I was wrong.

Out of bed around two this afternoon, I went downstairs to the lobby—and He was waiting inside the door. He still needed me. Waiting with the utmost concentration of a seemingly casual corner of the eye—for when my foot touched the final carpeted step, He was already turning, pressing His palms against the glass door to the street. I had come down for the breakfast they had refused to bring to my room owing to the lateness of the hour. Yet I followed. The boulevards were hot and crowded. The meaning of what I had seen last night now seemed to be not what I imagined. Or last night He made no demands, while now He was calling for the sacrifice of my breakfastless time. Not really that—I might have said no—but didn't—and even He might have been without His breakfast, He did walk more slowly, perhaps unsteadily, pausing now, frequently even, to study shop windows which, with the one exception, He had largely ignored last night on the long boulevards radiating from the central square, windows into which He now looked, indeed peered with a special intensity lacking from the pinched faces of the bumping, shoving cellulose crowd—at, oddly, enlarged sanitary backdrop photographs in camera stores, at cameras, radios, tape recorders, television sets, at, oddly, the stiffened taxidermies of clothing stores, at the flashing covers of magazines which hung by corners like game birds, feathers fingered by the breeze—as if in the crowd of shoppers, whose clothes and shoes alone made noises, there was not one face which promised, spoke—whispered—as much as any one face on paper that just came fresh from the printer's, a hundred thousand (a million?) copies, predictable of utterance, true friend (or lover)—who tells all—but can be told nothing, the half-people, who enslave, who are a currency, who drive mad and, above all, are never there. Or, in all this starting and stopping before plate glass, in which I found it impossible to maintain that fixed and perfectly calculated distance between us—death by newspaper—was an admission that the game was without honor, for of course it was a game, but a game engaged upon with the tacit understanding that it was blessed with a transcendent meaning, and now perhaps He was confessing that it was only a game, a hermetically enclosed sphere, that He led, that I followed, neither more nor less, that there had been no rendezvous last night, or no one left to come to it but me, watching, that there had been no one in that suburban house at dawn, that He was in search of only one thing, one person, pure and sterile, which was Himself searching, and that my following served only to give currency to His search. He wanted to be arrested in movement, held, photographed in the pose of search, He was borrowing my eyes to see Himself thus, He was not really searching for her, He was searching for someone to watch him— try. And He had found me. That was all He wanted. A certificate of sentimental behavior, issued by my intense stare. No, I would be there no longer, I would stare no more, and I quickened my step; I would catch up with Him, grab Him by the shoulder and finally have the whole truth out; there would be a scene, the police would come, they would tell me.

Yet the crowd, which might have been coming to life, was thickening and I lost Him around a corner: to the central square. The neon man, now bleached by the sun, walked ever stiffly, a fool, above a throng in the square; and beyond the bushes over the public toilet, almost opposite the cafe where we sat last night, a mammoth tent, stained to grey, now stood, snapping bright banners at the wind and string-drawn crowds. Traversing a brief opening in the traffic, He walked around the bushes and into the crowd before the tent, where I lost sight of Him against my own will, a first and most painful time. Now I crossed. At the opening of the tent a tangle of people pushed in and out, whispered, heads all turned towards the interior—where I was soon drawn, dragged, shoved, into an unbearable heat. The light of the sun burning through the tent fabric cast all forms into almost unrecognition, making shadows hot and of more dimension than those who cast them, and He or no one quite distinct was to be made out amongst the crowd of perhaps a thousand seated in folding chairs and milling up and down the aisles, and this had to be an end, I could not bear this, not any more, not the heat, the crush, not a loudspoken melodramatic voice booming over oleaginous anointments of an electric organ, not life-size plastic dummies with zip-on faces, not the headless crowd switching between watching and wanting to escape the oppressive heat, not an electromechanical household tombstone, I travel too much to be able to use one. Suddenly I was free, outside, gasping the freshest of airs. How close I had been to passing out!—being trampled—stuffed—mechanized—sold—senseless, or being torn to pieces by the thousand-eyed crowd, stolen bit by bit, until nothing more than a core, a shell of something which I could not guess, of a nakedness which only I could not see; and the sweating mob was pushing in and out of the tent, and still I could hear the voice proclaiming once-in-a-lifetime introductory offer reductions. I travel too much to be able to use one. I rinsed my face under a nearby fountain. Drops splashing into the water, I waited a time. But He was no longer to be seen. There or anywhere.

And soon it was time to resume my way.

✦

The train is laboring up the side of a ridge, wheels screaming and couplings a-clank, and from this elevation New Curío City is a brown smear against the valley floor. There was something irreversible or unrepeatable about my departure—a seemingly ordinary one: taxi to train station, then to the first-class compartment I had reserved all to myself—though I am not sure what it is, unless it be the other side of a feeling that New Curío City is the last of its kind I shall ever see, and that my destination is a place from which I will never return. Or that I have forgotten something, left something behind and cannot think what.

No, no, of course I will return to New Curío City. It is large, and it lies in the way. And it is in some sense—and this I feel—where I live.

The jostling of the train makes writing difficult, even those quick little jabs I make and which are indecipherable except by my closest of former friends. The train was held up three hours on the valley floor by an automobile accident at a crossing. I am having lunch served in my compartment. I have been with people all day. I have no desire to see any more of them.

✦

Once over the ridge, the train entered upon a high plateau, virtually unpopulated and marked only by low-lying vegetation, neither green nor brown, an occasional boulder, a rare knoll and in the very far distance a purple range of mountains. Several hours we rode at a slow pace across this flat, high land, which seemed to expand interminably, until reaching a sort of settlement, where the train stopped. This was it, the gateway to my next destination, which was to be the Ruiñs.

This being the off-season, I was the only passenger to dismount from the thirty-car train, and I watched it glide away, around a bend towards another point on the plateau, with all the satisfaction of an anticipated solitude. There was no one here, no life, no transportation, only a sort of dump that stretched several miles west and which had to be crossed, this time of year, on foot. I picked up my suitcase and stepped over the tracks. I soon came on to a footpath, and though it had not been used recently the serpentine depression worn in the sand by thousands of tourists was still distinct enough to follow, and it was probably the most efficient way through the forests of barbed wire that bordered the tracks, and beyond, great earthworks, concrete bunkers, artillery emplacements and all manner of fortifications that lie around most sides of the Ruiñs.

The path went up and down in a pleasing manner, around bomb craters or sometimes right across the center of them, then up to cross a concrete slab between great cannons turning to rust, around a hasty cemetery strewn with helmets and rifles, their wooden stocks long-since rotted away, until the plateau regained its flatness, the fortifications ran out and now there was only a great forest of machinery, so thick that the path became a crooked white line bordered by sands stained completely to rust. Fleets of ancient tanks, trucks, cannons of all sizes, skeletons of canvasless airplanes, mounds of spent cartridges, stacks of fuel barrels, wire, telephones and paper turned to pulp by decades of rain. A short armored train sporting a huge mortar, now leaning to one side on tracks half-buried by the sand. A thicket of tent poles. And faded uniforms, once bright, peeping cuffs and collars and buttons from shallow burials.

The path entered a clearing, then led up to a slight rise, to a sort of crest, where lay toppled a great billboard bearing the inscription, DO NOT TOUCH. A few steps beyond I came to the edge of a steep slope, almost a cliff, and there I paused to survey below the extensive valley which held the magnificent expanse of the Ruiñs. I admired the breathless panorama at some length, I sat and rested some, and finally I began the long, rocky descent.

※

The Ruiñs are of sufficient renown that I need not make a lengthy description of them, except perhaps of those peculiarities that have not hitherto been remarked by even the most meticulous of observers. What new thing could I possibly say about these glorious monuments to a past age? These wonders of primitive engineering? These masterpieces of art which lie upon the very doorsteps of the houses of those ancient but vanished people? Who am I to criticize the manner of archaeological restoration? No, the only new fact that I can communicate in all humility to the armchair traveler is that the Ruiñs are now being visited by myself, a unique historical event whose significance is not for me to comment upon, far from it.

At least I am not having to rough it here. The hotel on the hill overlooking the Ruiñs is closed for this part of the year, but while poking around the Ruiñs I was lucky enough to stumble upon the house of the janitor, in whose guest room I am now resting up. Although he was out maintaining the extensive grounds and may not be back for several days, his charming wife issued me a three-day visitor's permit. It is not widely known, I believe, that the janitor actually owns the Ruiñs, which he inherited some time before the war and which have been in the family—in part at least—since the foundation of the ancient city; and when he dies they will pass into the hands of his two sons, now away somewhere. The number of tourists who come here is strictly limited by decree; the janitor prefers to support his family and the maintenance work by means of royalties from the numerous well-illustrated volumes about the Ruiñs available throughout the world. He has in fact, his wife said, little time to show people around the Ruiñs, once inhabited by over a hundred thousand people who built as far as the eye could see. Discreetly I inquired into the cause of abandonment—plague, volcanic ash, massacre, crop failure, etc.—and she replied with a smile, wiping her hands on an apron, that the Ruiñs were not so much abandoned as bought up—a startling revelation. Our little talk took place all over the house, for when I arrived she was in the process of cleaning up something of a mess—hundreds of glasses, choked ashtrays, crumpled napkins, spent matches, crackers, confetti. (Whether this was the aftermath of a party the night before, or the effect of a special style of living, I could not then determine.) It seems that her husband's grandfather bought out the whole town and then expelled everyone. The last resident left about thirty-five years ago, taking the train, she thought, for her father-in-law complained frequently about there being one missing. Train, she meant, excusing herself for having so much work to do and being unable to sit down and chat in an orderly manner. Not at all, I protested, following her around the house, a single-storey dwelling composed of a variety of wings, comfortable and well-furnished. One wing contains the master bedroom and guest room with a modern bathroom at the end of the hall, while a second wing houses a sizable living room, a third the dining room and kitchen and there is another wing with more bedrooms and a second bath, but now closed up. To the back of the house is an immense garden, lush in vegetation and well kept. With the exception of the guest room, the house is lavishly hung, indeed crowded, with works of art taken from the Ruiñs and of no mean interest; and the whole establishment exhibits a pleasant intermingling of botany and art. I was especially taken by a portrait of the janitress nude and reclining on a bed of blue flowers, of a style somewhat primitive, which hangs in the dining room. Yet she was not entirely happy with the house. Too small she said, especially compared to what they might live in elsewhere in the Ruiñs if they chose to, and she was willing. But her husband refused to move. For him the house wasn't so important, since he was always outside fiddling around with his things. That was the trouble, she sighed.

Though charming she might be, though quick to smile and long to hold it, though fetchingly dressed in a deep lavender skirt and multi-blue blouse, she seemed to be a very discontented woman.

I soon retired to the guest room where I am now lying in its hard and narrow bed, which is as I prefer. The room is remarkable mainly for its plainness, with the exception of the wallpaper's flamboyant pattern of flowers, feminine in tone and no doubt chosen by the janitress herself; otherwise, I say, the room is plain and almost spartan. And almost primitive, for like the others it is fitted for electricity (and the kitchen for water and gas) but everything seems to have fallen into disuse or have been disconnected. The modern—but waterless, lightless—bathroom is outside the door, just down the hall a few steps. From my window one can peer through the holes in the shrubbery and see down the street towards the center of the Ruiñs, that once busy hub; and the street itself could pass for a well-kept lawn or mall were it not for two interminable rows of ancient vehicles rusting at the curbs, on flattened tires and, protruding through the grass, some still-polished streetcar tracks, a loose paving brick.

⁂

I was mistaken.

I had just rolled over to take a nap when the ceiling lamp, a high-powered unshaded bulb, went on. A curious phenomenon. The light bulb is undoubtedly older than I am. Now from outside the window came an ominous rumble. I propped myself up in bed and saw an ancient though freshly painted streetcar wallowing down the tracks. It stopped before the house and a man got out and walked past my window towards, I assumed, the front door. A moment later the janitress started shouting, and perhaps for me, so I shed my orange bathrobe for my white linen suit and went down the hall past an interesting collection of photographs and drawings to the living room. The man turned out to be her husband, the janitor and—at first glance—something of a bastard. Green of eye and gold of hair, his face bore an expression (permanent, it would seem) of sullen, inner wrath, which suggested a capacity for infinite grudge, and I noticed he was none too steady on his feet. From perhaps a nervous condition or overwork. Right before me he gave her a dressing down for issuing me the three-day pass. She argued that they hadn't had a tourist in two months now and could use the money. These passes are expensive, as you know. Now he informed me coldly that the price of admission did not include a service charge, obligatory, fifty per cent more. I paid it reluctantly on the spot; he stuffed the money into his pocket and told me that it was absolutely prohibited to visit the Ruiñs unescorted, either by day or by night, for there was a looter running around town and I was liable to be shot at—or shot.

Did he mean, I asked, that I was under suspicion?

Yes, that's exactly what he meant.

This appeared to be a most chilling reception. Or the man was starved. Lunch was now served in their ample dining room, a delicious lunch of silence broken only by my apt and regular compliments on the cooking, which the janitress received with long, wordless smiles. Suddenly over coffee the janitor slapped his palms on the table and confessed that maintaining the Ruiñs was a tiresome job and that he longed to be free of it and become a footloose traveler—like myself. The intensity of his stare (at me) made it clear that here was not a matter to be taken lightly; indeed, his wife now twisted herself up with a bitter sob and said, half crying, that they couldn't leave or even think of it, for here was their only home, their ancestral property where they had everything they wanted, and they couldn't possibly give it up even if their responsibilities ended up killing them. If this was a quarrel, it was as soon over and forgotten. With a kiss to her husband, she cleared the table and asked him to please make the water run so she could do the dishes, and while he was at it he could show me part of the Ruiñs. He grunted and stood up from the table, slipped on an old leather jacket and took a shotgun down from the wall, now gestured for me to follow him out the door.

We boarded the streetcar, which had been turned into a machine shop and was filled with power tools and stacks of scrap lumber and metal, and set off. The passing scene was of the greatest interest and of some intricacy. For reasons which still remain obscure we passed the house twice on the way to where we were going. Yet all praise to the innumerable splendid multi-storeyed structures a style peculiar to the area, of wood, stone, brick and handsomely draped with mosses and vines and sprouting trees and the spectacular patterns of innumerable DO NOT TOUCH signs, each painted in a different style. Many roofs were fallen in. There was no glass left in any of the windows. (It appeared that a number of plywood panels in the back of the trolley were destined as window covers.) Now and then the janitor stopped to kick a balcony railing, a drainpipe, or some other fixture blown from the Ruiñs, off the tracks.

A grey stone building of no mean architectural interest, some eight or nine storeys high, proved to be the destination. Parking before it, the janitor walked to the back of the trolley and cleared some hand tools off two large steel trunks, one of which contained thousands of keys, the other as many or more key tags bearing realistic photographs of keys. I feared this might be it. What? That little task that can drive one into a rash act. Never mind. The janitor, dextrous of finger and concentrated of mind, succeeded in matching key tag and key in less than twenty minutes and, more important, the key was the one that fitted the door to the grey stone building. (A forest of sycamore-like trees clutched its façade.) We went inside. Into a damp and total gloom. The janitor lit a stubby candle and we walked for some distance, finally reaching an enormous valve with an ornate circular handle. He stuck the candle on the bolt in the center of the handle and gestured to me to help him turn it clockwise. It was indeed stiff turning. He had said not a word since leaving the house, but now suddenly he blurted out that his wife had a lover. *Here?* In the Ruiñs? Yes, he gasped, and we panted through its maximum of three turns, while off in the great cavern of a building a slow dripping of water started.

After lighting a cigarette, he explained that the water couldn't be left on owing to the poor condition of the Ruiñs' pipes: already, even with only five minutes a day, the principal boulevard was turning into a marsh. The utilities problem, as he called it, actually consumed most of his time. The year before he had been forced to shut down the gas works altogether after a series of explosions, and he had still not got around to draining all the gas off the works and until such time as he did it would be dangerous to smoke in the Ruiñs (as he was now, however). I asked about electricity. He replied that it was turned on only when he used the trolley and that a special line ran from the overhead wires into the house, so that the wife could have some light now and then. No other buildings were connected. The amazing sewer system, an early triumph of engineering, was still intact and I could see it any time I liked—even alone. I told him not today. I had my white linen suit on.

He checked his watch and said his wife should have enough water now for the dishes, and we closed the valve and went back outside.

From there we took the trolley down the street to the central square, which was planted with a thick forest of fir-like trees, then turned right and went down a wide avenue of knee-high grass. A few blocks later he stopped the trolley and excused himself to do a little work. Taking a scythe from the pile of tools, he set about mowing around a block's worth of the avenue, and during those hours, perhaps most of the afternoon, I paced back and forth on the remains of a sidewalk until, somewhat weary, I removed a DO NOT TOUCH sign from a park bench and dozed in the sun to the cheepings of innumerable birds. When he was finished mowing, he raked the cuttings into neat piles and threw them over an iron fence around a huge mansion or villa where lived a sizable herd of pigs.

On the way back to the house, he made a brief stop to shoot a pheasant-like creature in a weed-choked alley.

I presume it will be for dinner.

But this day remains flawed by the fact that I was unable to visit the Ruiñs alone. Really we saw very little of them and went by much too fast. Or—and this too is possible, though I hesitate to believe it—perhaps I have seen most of the Ruiñs after all. I cannot really know. Decay (which exposes) renders everything familiar, intimate, and one is cheated out of any precise discovery by the overwhelming revelation. I speak of the small corner one stumbles across all alone. And which becomes—flaming out of proportion—the most valuable. But I am to be dressed for dinner.

Now.

I went downstairs to find the janitress executing the final basting upon the roast pheasant-like bird, in appearance a true masterpiece of cookery and of fragrance sublime. She said her husband was in his room reading newspapers and would be out in a while. Newspapers? Old newspapers he picked up during his maintenance tours, yes, and that was all he read nowadays. Talking did not seem to hinder her intricate basting gestures, and she went on to say that she had urged him many times to find out where the public library was—and there was one around as his great-grandfather had endowed it—but he wouldn't be bothered, even for her sake. That was one of their problems. And there were others. (She was speaking, still bent over the range, with a rapidity that could not be called prudent.) Such as? Mainly keeping herself amused during the off-months when there were no tourists, one problem of a seasonal, circular life. I quite agreed. What she and her husband wanted to do was to get out of the tourist business altogether—excepting present company (me)—for which they would have to be self-supporting first. Then they could have just their personal friends here as guests, and all year round. The Ruiñs, though often impenetrable for weeks on end, were the most beautiful under a heavy blanket of snow. But in order to drop the tourist trade, they needed an independent income twice what they now had from the picture-books about the Ruiñs, which in fact they hoped to withdraw from circulation some day also. The less known about the Ruiñs, the better. I expressed oblique surprise at their money worries. Were they not in fact amongst the wealthiest people of this particular continent? Not at all, she said, shoving the bird back into the oven, they were amongst the poorest, for her father-in-law, having invested his entire fortune in the town, had left them only the cash equivalent of about three dollars in small change. She remembered the day. As was their custom the first of every month, they went over to his house, the most splendid mansion in town, to pay their respects over a cup of tea, and there they found him dead (of unknown causes) in his armchair, his last will (Would I like to see it? No.) neatly laid out on a coffee table and weighted down by an old sock containing the coins.

Yes, I agreed, it was something of a pathetic end. Silently I wondered why I was being told all these things. She moved around the kitchen, from stove to sink to table, pot to pan, chopping, stirring, beating, with a grace beyond description, as in a dance of perfectly harmonious domesticity. Aside from such incidents, she said, it was really a delightful place to live—calm, peaceful, solitude. Only one thing did she dread, fixing me with an intense stare not unlike her husband's, and that was when they quarrelled. He always went off to the railway station to sulk. Three miles away. And they might not see each other for an entire month. Did this happen often? No. Very rarely. But when he went off like that she had to stay in the house alone and couldn't go outside, since the wife of the leading citizen could not afford to be seen alone on the streets, which were not safe anyway, and she had never learned to drive the streetcars. Only once did she dare leave the house— she was so angry—to take refuge in the principal hotel where she tried to starve herself to death; but in the end she went delirious and by accident they met in the central square, she wasting away and he nearly unrecognizable behind a bushy red beard, and they made it up right there, amongst the fir-like trees. But when their sons came back from wherever they were, things would be easier for them all—*if* they came back, she sighed, for that was another problem, there were so many problems now, and she was counting so much on their following in their father's footsteps. (Where?) Yes, I agreed, it would indeed be tragic if they decided to sell off the Ruiñs: once these things leave the family, there is no getting them back. But she said it was a delightful place to live—calm, peaceful, of a solitude.

Did I want to buy them?

What?

The Ruiñs. She could make a very attractive price for me. The husband need not know, of course.

I said I thought not, but would give it my earnest consideration. Perhaps another time.

Night fell and the janitor thundered into the living room carrying a brown newspaper, tattered and worm-eaten. His wife now excused herself to go change for dinner and I joined the husband in the living room where he began reading the newspaper aloud in a booming voice. Without asking me. It was, he commented in frequent asides, a choice specimen. An ancestor of his was mentioned prominently in every news item, be it of court proceedings to evict other inhabitants, or lists of businesses and industries closing down, or bloody strikes and street violence, assassinations. Until the newspaper disintegrated between his hands. He threw the scraps into the fireplace and turned to me and said that he had overheard that I had been talking to his wife in the kitchen. I said yes, that was correct. In that case, he said, I should keep a few things in mind. Gladly. She could be a dangerous and irresponsible woman. Really? I should not be deceived by her charming manner, her long warm smile, her apparent competence around the house (and she was a good mother without a doubt), for behind these pleasant externals the fact could not be denied that she had never had the background required to inhabit the Ruiñs in the proper style. She was too fond of unnecessary people. She was easily bored, quick to hysteria—qualities which could be fatal in a place as demanding as this. Nor was he reproaching her for being the way she was, since these things had not stopped him from marrying her, as he had done at the risk of his father's disapproval and disinheritance, which would have meant expulsion from the Ruiñs; he was only saying that he was getting all the hell from her, neither more nor less, that he deserved. I said I was having trouble grasping the point. He explained. He was of an ancient and titled family of hermits who propagated themselves through random and often rash acts of copulation and he, the present janitor, was the first in family memory not to have his wife or mistress done away with upon the production of a healthy heir. I see. Indeed, I saw; what with her blue eyes and black hair and pleasing round forms, not only was it clear that she had come from another family, but from another race or region as well. Yes, he carried upon him the burden of having broken with family tradition. Now (and he had me by the lapel) would I please render him a service. I replied that to the best of my ability I would render him any service not inconsistent with my own beliefs, which, he would find, were few and far between. He asked, reaching over with his free hand and opening a desk drawer which contained some false hair, a sort of mask and a small pistol, he asked me whether I might like to disguise myself and break into the house—at any hour of my choice—and fire the gun. And he winked.

I winked back but said nothing. This man was clearly a threat.

She now made her appearance in a light-blue gown that could only be described as formal, and to his look of consternation she said softly with a long smile that it was Saturday night. We ended up eating our dinner in absolute silence after the failure of my attempts to enliven the gathering with apt remarks on the tastiness of the food, the simple but elegant table setting and so forth. The pheasant-like bird was indeed the most delicious cooked creature I have ever eaten on my travels. The argument broke out over coffee. He said he would not go out. She said it was Saturday night and they hadn't been out for three months now and their visitor—myself—would be cheated if he couldn't see the Ruiñs by night when they were especially beautiful. I went pooh-pooh, as it were, between them. He roared across the table that he was tired after a hard day's work. He only wanted to go to bed. Wouldn't she ever realize that going outside at night was the most dangerous thing they could do? And their evenings out in the Ruiñs were always so boring. I tried to look incredulous. Well that was his fault, she cried, and after all they both had to make little sacrifices now and then, and all she wanted was to get out of the house where she was cooped up all day preparing it for the hours when he came home, so he could be comfortable and have a real home—and if he wouldn't go out this evening she would ask their charming, affable, handsome visitor (myself) to escort her. Did I carry a gun. No, never.

All right, he thundered, disappearing out the front door.

She gave me a wan smile and cleared the table. A few minutes later the lights went on (we had eaten by candlelight), followed by the squeaky halt of a streetcar outside, and now the janitor appeared at the door, a shotgun slung over his shoulder and a wild look in his eye. As soon as she was finished in the kitchen, we locked up the house and boarded the trolley; this one, an elegant private car, was fitted out as an oak-panelled lounge-bar and featured hand-woven carpets and massive armchairs and a liberal supply of an ancient brandy, which the wife and I sipped while the janitor worked at the controls.

We set off and, in clanking passage, gained the principal boulevard under a night clear and cloudless and of a full moon, which cast a blue frost upon façades, trees, vines and the thousands of vehicles, while low down the trolley's yellow beam washed over innumerable blades of misted grass and thin shiny rails, across which scurried grey forms from one darkness to another. We reached the entrance to the central square within a few minutes. The janitor stopped the trolley. After a moment of silence, there rose the cries of hundreds of nocturnal birds, into almost a scream, to be drowned out then by a lugubrious howling, clear-throated and higher and higher, which came, it seemed, from a pack of dog-like creatures crouching with red eyes under the forest of fir-like trees. The janitor swore, then thrust his shotgun out a window and fired a solitary blast. The animal sounds chokingly subsided into another silence, shadowed only by distant echoes of the explosion, mumbling back down the radial boulevards.

We continued to the other side of the central square, alighting before a drooping marquee. Here they had another quarrel. He had not remembered to bring the key along. She told him, finger quivering, to break that door down. It was in fact about to fall apart of its own accord. Nor did he have any candles. She laughed, produced five from her purse. He swore and threw aside a DO NOT TOUCH sign and kicked the door in. Candles lit, we passed through a lobby to the main hall of what appeared to be a large theatre or opera house. Strange breezes of varying temperatures circulated from most every direction, and from the darkness above, touched only by a line of gilt, perhaps of a balcony, there came waves of soft sounds, rustlings and scratchings, perhaps a hiss. After walking about three-quarters of the way down the aisle towards the stage, the janitor motioned me towards a seat and we sat down while his wife went on ahead with all the candles.

Within a few minutes the stage was illuminated, though dimly, and I could make out the sets of what appeared to be an operatic kitchen laid upon a perspective acutely reversed. Of stretched canvas, for they quivered as she walked around. The center piece, placed in the background and measuring some twelve feet to a side, was an operatic electric range which served almost as a backdrop. To its left towards the foreground stood a great white operatic refrigerator, smaller than the range, which adjoined a sharply diminishing and somewhat tilted sink and drainboard; while right center foreground was taken up by a table and four chairs. These last were small, suitable only for dwarfs. And other things, of size and arrangement such that the janitress, as she walked around, seemed to change size herself, looming large in the foreground, becoming tiny in the background. Which, upon reflection, is not so extraordinary.

She now pulled from behind the operatic range a number of flat painted figures. Cut from plywood or something of that nature, and fitted with heavy circular bases, their painted clothes and features were of a childlike simplicity and uniformity that made them practically indistinguishable one from another. There were seven men of blank, simpleton expressions, and who varied only slightly in stature, and three women who had no heads at all. (The janitress was later to stand behind them in such a way that only her neck and head showed above the flat figures.) After arranging the figures on the stage, she disappeared out the left wing.

The janitor now told me to applaud. I did so—until drowned out by a frightful commotion overhead as hundreds, perhaps thousands of pigeons and bats broke into noisy flight. Though I could have sworn there was someone else applauding in that darkness. The janitress now walked onstage and bowed, and when the pigeons were quiet she began. I will not praise her stunning figure here— she was nude—as she soon disappeared behind the cutouts.

The janitor promptly fell asleep and set to snoring so loudly that I found it almost impossible to make out what she was saying. What the play was about. Yet a seemingly impressive performance, and I cannot praise too highly her gestures, for one. As for the rest, I cannot say. One gesture in fact was directed right at me, perhaps in the middle of the second act when she went suddenly silent and beckoned me up on the stage. So that I might hear better, I thought. But she took me by the arm and drew me behind one of the men-figures and started whispering so excitedly that I found it difficult to follow her at first. Something about wanting me to join a conspiracy. Her lovers were all here in the theatre. *Now?* Yes she said they were a resistance group made up of ex-post office employees, close to forty in number, whose base of operations was the outbuilding of a suburban villa rarely visited by the janitor. Her husband, I reminded her. Of course. But while their principal concern was getting the mail through, they had come of late to see the desirability of seizing the post office building. Then they would launch a full-scale uprising to restore the Ruiñs to its original continental prominence. Would I help? Frankly, I whispered, I couldn't see myself, a professional traveler, becoming tied up in what really looked like a property scheme, as I travel too much to need land, and so forth. Though, of course, my utter confidence she could be assured of. She was holding me very close now. Would I at least *give*? What? They collected stamps. By all means, I said, removing a packet of letters from my coat and ripping off a dozen colorful stamps. There, she said, pointing around the man-figure and downward. I peeked, and there in the orchestra pit, all huddled together, grubby, ill-shaven and eyes bloodshot, were all her lovers. So on the way back to my seat and the still-sleeping janitor, I let the stamps fall into the pit, into their outstretched hands, their trembling fingers, a memorable scene.

The performance then resumed, and lasted a few more hours.

❖

Sunday morning the household was ablaze with argument. She wanted to go out, he wanted to stay in, he wouldn't let her go out alone. She ran out the door and taunted him from the front lawn. He raised his shotgun (unloaded) and pulled the trigger. She fainted. I ran to my room and locked the door, refusing to be a party to this nonsense, and went to bed, where I reflected on the sad fact that my three-day pass would waste away unused at this rate, and was more like a ticket to prison. For how could I leave with things like this?

A scratching at the window-screen brought me to my feet. I went over to the window and peered out. It was the janitor, bent over, eyes shaded with his hands, looking right in at me. Fortunately he no longer had the gun, or had at least left it in the bushes. I asked him how things were going. Awful, he replied. In fact he was afraid he had a full-blown quarrel on his hands. I asked if there was anything I could do. He coughed and shuffled around a bit, then whispered through the screen. Could I please leave? What, now? I asked. Yes, right now, he said. He thought it would be, frankly, the best thing. As long as there was going to be a quarrel he might as well make it a real production and there would be no place for me in it unless I were willing to take sides. To be blunt, was I? I appreciated this honesty and said no. Quite all right, he said, so long as I permitted him to blame the janitress for driving me off I thought it wise to make this concession, and did so. And he vanished through the bushes.

But the doorknob was already twisting and turning. I crossed the room and slid back the latch, whereupon the janitress burst in, gasping for breath. Now did I see what a terrible man her husband was? Yes, I said, I thought she had a point. At least he was dangerous enough. But at this, oddly, she laughed, then said that she thought the Ruiñs were not really the place for me at the present moment, that is, because she had a certain respect for me, she would prefer that I not be around when she took care of her husband. It would not be pleasant. But it was now necessary. Did I agree? Yes, I thought something ought to be done but could not commit myself to anything in particular—and I was leaving this very instant.

Which I repeated feignedly for the benefit of the janitor, who had just walked through the door. His gun clattered to the floor. Suddenly back into domestic harmony, they (or 'we', to quote) were already sad to have me go so soon, when would I be back to see them again, what could they do to soften the hardships of my journey, please send them a postcard at least, or better a long letter; and she rushed off to the kitchen while he, tugging me by the cuff, took me out the front door and led me a few blocks away to a warehouse-like structure. Inside were some fifty vehicles similar to those in the streets, but in excellent condition, neither rotting nor rusting, and on the spot he presented me with a bright red roadster, ancient of vintage and distant of origin. As a rule I do not drive and thus know nothing about these things, but to judge from the lengthy starting time and silence of operation the automobile was powered by steam. The janitor had me drive it around a few blocks to teach me the purpose of the pedals and levers and knobs and the meanings of the gauges, and told me innumerable things I was *not* to do, separately or simultaneously, if I desired *not* to be blown to pieces.

No sooner had we stopped before the house, before its handsome stone-cut DO NOT TOUCH sign, than the janitress dashed from it to hand me a huge basket of food, adding interminable wishes for a happy journey, and now her husband raced in and out of the house with my suitcase, which required, I imagine, no little effort to pack. The janitor climbed back into the roadster and as soon as I had bid the janitress goodbye, we set off. To the outskirts of the Ruiñs, I assumed, where I would leave him. But now he informed me that he was going along. Where? With me, on my travels. His admiration for my way of life was unbounded, and he wished now to do only one thing: to imitate it in my presence. Furthermore, he confessed, he had become very fond of me. He could not bear the idea of parting. He would never go back there. I listened to this and more in silence, then said, with utter frankness, that the untidy way with which he was leaving his home did not inspire me to believe that he would make a well-mannered traveling companion, and that the probability that we too would have a falling out, sooner or later, was just too great. And, of course, the consequences would be doubly disastrous. So I advised him to stay. Perhaps another time. The world was always there to be seen, and I was always going around it.

In the end, he accepted his fate, and even extended an invitation to return. Most certainly I would. We parted then at the edge of the Ruiñs, where the street ended in a dirt road, and as he climbed into an awaiting trolley, I switched the roadster from low to medium and sped off into a barren countryside.

⸙

The road being rough and the car poorly sprung, I drove slowly and with some deliberation across what soon became an interminable plain which, though flat in appearance from a distance, proved to be cut by countless gullies and small canyons, and the road wound in and out of them in a most inefficient manner, reducing my progress to nothing compared with what I had hoped. I feared also for the machine. Were it to break in any manner I would be stranded with no one to repair it or tap the questionable resources of the countryside; and skeletons lined the road. A barren, hostile country, relieved only by low-lying grey brush and smooth round boulders in whose shadows grew a tiny blue flower of a variety I have never seen before; and a soundless country too, beyond a soft regular ticking of the engine, the crunch of tires on gravel, or a stray gust of wind reaching down from the sky and beating against the windshield.

The horizon ahead was graced by a solitary range of purple mountains floating above a thin line of haze, which might have been a mirage. The Resørt, if I remembered correctly, lay just to the other side. And above the purple range hung the pale diaphanous disk of an almost full moon, rising perhaps, while the sun was falling from its point of noon. I was heading west, the preferred direction of my travels. The purity of the desolation soon wore away my worries about the machine. Of solitudes, a moving solitude is the finest. Bushes grow into focus, now slip out the sides of the windshield, and one compares them in size with each other, with perhaps an idealized bush; and the same for boulders, for the width of the twisting road, the rocks that have fallen into it, the tones of the blue sky which are deepest straight up and fade towards the horizons: all an exercise of the faculties of perception for the pure pleasure of it and without nagging utility, for I had nothing to do with this landscape but to cross it, and in so doing look at it, since, with the first feeling of confidence, I was now able to exclude from my mind the possibility of the machine breaking down. It would not happen. A greater possibility was the landscape itself breaking down, so to speak—turning suddenly into mud, powder, or paper.

While rising from one of the innumerable gullies, I came upon a woman standing at the side of the road. Dressed in a simple manner, her face was covered up to the eyes with a white veil. I examined her the best I could with the car jiggling, as I might an odd road sign in a foreign language out in the middle of nowhere, and drove on. I was enjoying the scenery too much to be bothered by the chatter of a hitchhiker. However, several hundred yards later it occurred to me that I might become lonely, in particular if I did not reach the Resørt this evening. I stopped, turned around in the seat—there was no mirror—and squeezed the bulb horn three times. The machine, as the janitor had explained to me, was irreversible so there was nothing I could do but sit and wait for her to catch up. I passed the time by working on my notes.

She climbed in and we were off. The bouncing of the machine and the breeze through the open roof succeeded in detaching her veil, and now I recognized her as the one I might have referred to before as the Païnted Wōman, meaning of course the woman who uses makeup, neither more nor less. She was indescribably attractive. I cannot begin to list her beauties. Taking advantage of the silent operation of the machine, we engaged in conversation. She spoke very softly and smiled frequently. Her teeth were beyond compare—and real, I assure you. Her breath smelled of the finest of rare herbs. She too was a practitioner of the fine art of traveling, though in the opposite direction from myself, and had accepted my lift because she had become tired of waiting by the side of the road. We exchanged professional travelers' impressions on what we had seen, tips on where to stay or where not to, the best means of transportation from one point to the next, favorite foods. She admitted to a certain fatigue with this wandering life, and I likewise, though without denying the rewards of endless variety and the beneficial effects of constantly new experiences, which sharpen the mind and stabilize the heart. Though I confessed to a seeming unreality about my travels, which could not be helped, such was the world nowadays, invaded by a uniformity that threatened to make all places alike and the people the same everywhere, devoid of even national character; and often I felt like I was treading water, without advancement. She agreed. But, I added, there was no choice but to plunge on. She wanted to know why. Why not just stop? But that was something I could not answer and felt in fact that her 'why' was essentially unanswerable. That is, in so far as an answer is possible to any question, there was no answer. I explained to her charming smile that I much preferred to see the question as the fixed thing which must always remain a question, for in the answering of it, for in the attempt to answer it, one becomes swallowed up in the tangles of finite possibility, and I did not know of one thing which I could safely call finite, or fixed, or certain. I thought it a far better idea that she take back her question, lock it up, store it away, hold it, as she might a very precious momento, to be exhibited only on the most special of occasions, for one question, well and sparingly employed, will do the work of a thousand answers, none of them true for any time beyond the instant, so brief and fleeting, required to utter them. She could not but agree. At least she seemed to agree. Yet I could not be sure she entirely understood. I added one caution then, to the effect that what I had just said could be construed as the answer to a question from, say, out there, yonder, so that from another point of view I had made a mistake and had best retract my remark, to slip them back into the folds of silence. Which I would willingly do so long as she agreed to take back her question. Yes, she thought that to be the best solution.

We were close anyway to what might be called the 'hot-air point'. Neither of us was paying much attention to what we were saying. I was driving much too fast and tending to be forgetful about the curves, of the road. My hands began slipping from controls. She was overcome by a lassitude and stretched out. The fingers of her small hands were like the curling tendrils of a vine, searching to grasp. We were now at a perfectly flat area of the plain, which seemed endless, and the road extended like an orange ribbon to the purple mountains, now as distant as they had ever been. I stopped the machine. We were utterly alone.

We left the machine and walked away from the road into the plain, into the hollows of the softest of sands, virginal, untrodden and marked at even intervals by symmetrical grey bushes in whose shadows the wind had dropped tiny pebbles and where now sleek lizards trembled at our passage. Ah, we were lavish! Around the spot I chose for our act of copulation, first I spread her blue blouse neatly over a bush, then her lavender skirt over a second, and so on with her brassiere, slip, panties and stockings, until they formed around us a half circle, which I now closed with my white linen coat, trousers and my underwear—the limp petals of our flowering conjugation. Thereupon we donned our respective contraceptive devices. She lay down on the warm sand. Her shapely limbs were as the sudden incarnation of imaginary lines colliding upon a perfectly white sheet of paper. I knelt, caressed them and thrust myself into their axis. And now, through movement of the small cylindrical extension of the sack of flesh which was my body, mine, inside the woman upon whose softly giving form I lay, the only surface of friction, the harsh and pure landscape—which yet penetrated a dimmed eye—rocked and twisted and turned a few degrees in all directions; indeed there was no question that from this point, the point where the piston butted against an elastic but ultimately ungiving end, around this point the earth moved, perhaps only ever so slightly, while our own movement unlocked the perfumed case of her body to reveal an industry by the sea, where odors feinted through layers to hollows to tunnels, down towards a final darkness; and I said through my teeth to her ear, through harsh pantings, that from here man emerged, dripping acrid chemicals, to spend a time touching his own body and all others before passing on to invent himself, towards illusion, the one thing he could possess, and here, now, I wanted to know why I had to spring from woman, why, could she tell me why? But she could only gasp out a 'why not?' Only that. There was no time, for we were nearing our perfectly simultaneous climax, and a volcano of the distant range erupted in flame and an earthquake split huge cracks across the smooth, flat plain; and our orgasm began and now leaped into spasms so frenetic that the last one was of such violence and the plunge so deep that the rebound flung me completely out of her, and I crashed to the ground ten feet away, where, panting on my back, I witnessed the slow eclipse of the sun by the moon.

At last I recovered sufficient strength to creep back to her sleeping form in the half-light of the eclipse, mounted her again and matched my breathing to hers, and we slept.

It was a sleep I cannot describe, for it was only and yet so much more than a procession of soundless, reddish warmth, with no vision beyond the showers of light produced by a closed eye blinking its lids automatically; as when one sees, or thinks one sees the eye itself in the process of feeding itself, repairing itself, puttering around, checking out the mechanism during this moment of respite, idly waiting for the moment when the lids will be parted and the startling though sometimes tiring show to resume.

Our soul is in the eye, and when we open it, it escapes and becomes the universe. You will see everything in the line diagram of a biology book.

I, aqueous humour.

The sun slid from behind the moon and wiped clear a chill that was beginning to come on the air, on capricious breezes swooping down and away like birds, and during the rest of the afternoon and that night and next morning, I do not know how many times we copulated but would smilingly agree to any figure short of infinity, no matter how outrageous, that might come into my mind. Yet we were but mortals and to while away those hours when one more caress might raise a blister, we walked in all our nudity about the plain and finally chose a spot which was well supplied with stones to erect two monuments to our act. Of these the first was the most laborious, being a phallus ten feet high, two feet in diameter, of stones held together and covered over by a composition consisting of an extremely adhesive clay to be found in the cracks opened by the earthquake and mixed with crushed twigs, and the entirety was reinforced at the base by two testicles of uneven size, around which we replanted a number of those grey bushes. And in the clearing left by the replanted bushes, we constructed, on the same scale though slightly more stylized, huge labia around a half-open vulva in which we deposited the prettiest of the many pebbles to be found around the plain. I cannot praise the monuments too highly, and if the traveler finds himself in these parts, he is advised to stop and examine them. Heading towards the Resørt beyond the mountain range, the phallus is clearly visible to the left of the road and cannot be missed as it is the only landmark within miles.

At last the time came to clothe our bodies bronzed by the sun and hardened with healthy exercise and resume our journey. Our clothes felt scratchy and binding, like parasites sapping the energy of touch; they were other people, yet we could not do without them. Only our shoes could we leave off. I lit a match and set the red roadster to boil. We took one long last look at our monuments, lost ourselves in a final embrace; the machine hissed and we drove off to its regular ticking sounds.

The road was straight for the plain was now perfectly flat. She slept, her head bouncing on my shoulder. There is a peculiar beauty in the purity of such a landscape. Perhaps it is in the individual grains of sand which, moving at anything faster than a walking pace, one cannot see, only sense. But stop, bend over, look at the ground and all is revealed. Were one to examine with utter minuteness an ordinary floor carpet, what marvels one would see! We approached by imperceptible degrees the purple range, and I was confident of reaching the Resørt on the other side by nightfall. My reservation for a single room had lapsed by now, but then we were two.

A few hours later she awoke and chatted sleepily, and at great length, about the sort of hotel room we needed. I was in perfect agreement. The Resørt—she had just come from there—would otherwise be an abomination which I myself knew from a previous visit some years ago. I generally keep away from such places but there was no way of avoiding this one, and we both needed baths and square meals. Just before the purple range, which now loomed close ahead, the first road sign appeared. A large wooden panel bearing the bright blue seal of the national tourist commission, it read:

## THE BEST THINGS IN LIFE ARE *FREE*

Indeed, we could not but agree. The signs now began to appear at regular intervals on the right side of the dirt road; their blue letters, painted in a variety of scripts on a white background, dazzled the otherwise empty space.

## WORK HARD AND YOU SHALL FIND HAPPINESS AND LOVE

Equally true, and commendably placed on this barren waste. She thought it an unusually good idea to put up these signs: they helped pass the time and distance for those who might find the drive tedious—not us, of course, as we were far from bored with each other.

## SECURE THE FUTURE WITH THE IDEALS OF YOUR YOUTH

Which again was unquestionable and unforgettable, the sort of exhortation which increases one's sense of well-being, and it inspired her with renewed warmth and I found the quality of my driving impaired with her poignant fondlings.

## SUNSETS ARE BEAUTIFUL

It was, in fact, getting towards late afternoon and we were entering the shadow cast by the purple range.

## THE HOME IS WHERE GOD RESIDES

But, as I am a professional traveler, this one did not so much apply to me; nonetheless it was an apt saying and she liked it, explaining that she had been married to a man who suffered from recurrent photisms of a particularly infectious nature and who was mentally cruel and neglectful of his duties as a husband. Gently did I inquire as to whether she herself might have contributed to this lamentable situation, and she replied that there was no doubt in her mind as to her absolute innocence.

## LIFE'S BLESSING IS FULFILMENT

She was, after all, only a woman, though, she said, the times demanded much more than to be a glamorous child-bearing creature, they required her as a woman to be less feminine and more masculine, and as such she required a man who was even more virile than ordinary—such as myself, she added, and rare were they in this world; in fact, the only thing for a true woman to do in these times was to engage in prostitution so that, through the collective experience, she might acquire the notion of virility so sadly lacking in any individual man; again excepting myself.

## WELCOME TO THE RESØRT

Which was the last sign before we entered the tunnel through the purple range. This tunnel is only seven feet long, that is, the thickness of the purple range, which is constructed of enormous steel plates riveted together and stood on end to attain a frosty height of over a thousand feet at the peaks. Countless guy wires hold it in place and thousands of holes drilled through the steel plates, but not visible to the naked eye, allow the wind to circulate in such a way that there is no danger of the range being blown over during storms. A truly admirable engineering feat, justifiably celebrated in song and dance.

We were immediately in the thick of the Resørt with its teeming crowds, its carousing holiday-makers, its picturesque streets which all converged upon an interminable beach, and towards that I carefully directed the machine, squeezing the bulb horn now and then to warn away a drunken pedestrian, until we reached the Resørt's largest and most expensive hotel.

To our delight they had a double suite with a view of the sea.

✦

I am in bed.

Resting up from the exhausting drive across the plain, and other things. Because of telltale bodily marks—which other tourists seem to pride themselves in sporting—neither of us will do any sea-bathing except by night. She is in the next room. I don't know what she's doing. This hotel is far less than it seems. Below my window, twenty-four hours a day, thousands of murmuring tourists shuffle up and down the seaside promenade; they do not stop except to lean, they stare, or seem to stare, from behind colored glasses—which a city ordinance requires to be worn at all times: without them one is subject to indecent exposure—they stare at the beach, at the mausoleums, tombs, cenotaphs and shrines the wealthy have built there, facing out to sea, at sunbathers sprawled out on the tops of tombs, at the new arrivals, untanned and shrinking, who cower in the shadows, at—what?

The effect of vast stretches of marble where sand ought to be is, in the end, only repugnant.

I close my shutters. They damp the noise. But my room is plagued by the cry of next door's whistling toilet. It refuses to be fixed. I suppose I shall have to register another complaint. I think she has a headache. The hotel is very old. This is something the experienced nose can smell even through the most extensive remodelling jobs. Yet its height of luxury includes suites with three bidets and dancing fountain showers with multi-colored illumination and an infinity of mirrors. But we did not choose one of those. My room is simple, indeed almost spartan, my bed hard and narrow such as I prefer and such as one would not expect to find in a hotel of this softness, so to speak. But they have everything. The wallpaper is the color of the ocean. Speckled blue. As is the carpet, though monotone, and the blanket on the bed. In truth we have stopped talking to each other, having exhausted all subjects of conversation. By agreement purely mutual. Which grew out of a brief altercation in which she refused to answer a simple question and I could only reply by refusing to answer one of hers. Why talk if we have nothing to say to each other? Last night she refused to go up the escalator another time, said she could walk up the stairs. I don't hold it against her. The escalator, which goes up only, is man-powered: ten youths with the skimpiest of towels wrapped around their muscular loins, with golden nameplates hanging from their necks by little chains, bare-footedly run a treadmill parallel to the escalator—and too close, some might say. One of them keeps trying to slip me a note each time I go up, but I shall have none of that nonsense here. I would report his name to the manager—as she wants me to do, she who doesn't know that I've already had several proposals from him over the telephone, which would be false economy. Really—she is ignorant.

✦

This morning we walked a mile down the promenade to the last tomb, then a ways farther to sunbathe. From there one obtains an excellent view of this side of the purple range which is not, as it were, a purple range at all but rather the form of an enormous nude woman reclining in a bed of blue flowers. Early morning, before the breezes clean away a mellow varnish of haze, is the best time to observe this phenomenal work whose year-round upkeep draws the finest talents from the Resørt's distinguished university faculties. She must of course be constantly repainted and, thanks to a computerized number grid not visible to the distant eye, not one single line or shade has been mis-painted for over ten years. Otherwise, the Resørt is most definitely second-rate. I might commend the very white sand of its beaches. And there is the main promenade, stretching for miles in either direction as far as the eye can see, and lined with shouting hawkers of ice cream cones, sunglasses, sandals, brass priapi, bikinis, assorted erotic paraphernalia about which I know nothing, and, to my discomfiture, gentlemen in white suits who flap mausoleum catalogues at all strollers showing signs of feebleness. Here and there a crowd will gather around a craftsman working over a sarcophagus, pitiably similar to so many already on the beach and so many more being carved up and down the promenade, all the same: side-panels cut with styled views of the promenade, with tourists prancing nude in high relief against a shallower backdrop of hotels, and beneath the woman of the purple range; supply and demand, and in this now sadly commercialized folk industry the ancient sense of fantasy remains only now in the slab tops, which are carved with a forest of knobs and points in order, I gather, to discourage living sunbathers.

On our way back we witnessed what must be called a funeral procession. One wonders what will happen in a few years when all the available beach space is taken up by the tombs. Then, perhaps, they will have to be stacked. But we joined a crowd of downy arms and legs gathered around an open sarcophagus which contained the body of an ancient dowager, in dark glasses, and which was being rolled across the promenade on logs to its final resting place on the beach, a narrow space between two other tombs. We did not wait around to see the fitting of the lid, she did not want to, by eight young men in black loincloths.

Singing some sentimental tune.

✢

That was the last walk we took together in this place, and it will be the last ever. Everything came out this evening. I had been expecting as much. She has shown a great interest in this notebook, more than in any other piece of my modest traveling equipment, but I failed to see that her seemingly polite concern about it was leading up to a flat demand to read it, made last night with all the tones of an ultimatum. Of course, I said, that was out of the question. She took this very badly. She would not accept any of my simple and clear reasoning about the matter, and no sooner was my back turned than she began searching around to find out where I had hidden it. Perhaps I am being excessive. I mean: I could tell that she was watching and waiting for that moment when it would be absolutely safe to turn my room upside down; so as a precaution, I warned her that she had best exclude the idea of ever finding and reading it. To which she said nothing. I added then, casually, that it was getting late and that we had best part for the evening (she was in my room, all this time) so as to have a good night's sleep against our departure tomorrow morning. I have had quite enough of the Resørt and am anxious to leave. And here, I thought, at least we would be in total agreement.

I was already in bed, and she standing near the nightstand, fingering a pile of magazines towards, as I knew and she suspected, my notebook concealed beneath them, when she said, no, she didn't want to leave tomorrow. Immediately I conceded another day. One more or less did not matter that much. Nor then, she said. I demanded when. Never, she replied, for she refused to go on traveling together any more. Why? She was, I fear, a bit vague. Something about my being too interested in the scenery, at her expense. I told her I wouldn't accept that as an excuse, because everybody is perpetually complaining about being neglected. What was she really driving at? Did I really want to know? Of course. She said, plunging deeper into the magazines, that it was impossible to have children under such circumstances, that is, traveling all the time. A woman needs a spot to have children. A nest. What, I asked her with some impatience, was the matter with the world? Nothing, she said, except with me around she never felt at home in it.

And she swept from my room with a flight of hands, of sobs and tears, and a thunderous slam of the door.

## III. As it Were

⁕

With the disappearance of my notebook, I turned to the only writing material at hand, some large sheets of paper I found in the desk drawer and which I shall continue to use until this whole matter is cleared up. Now that I am released, if ever I was in custody, I am once again free to rest up from the ordeal. The sedatives I have been given are ineffective—police sedatives are, I find—but that doesn't matter. But it is all over, or seems to be.

I am weary of it—everything.

I have been so tired lately that I probably didn't notice, or care, when we moved from a hotel to a rented suburban villa, in one of whose bedrooms I am now lying. But I made the concession: we would stop traveling and stay in one spot for a time. But let us get to the facts without my opinions which in the end are only so much decoration that the so-called reader of this guide may choose to do without. The villa is tastefully furnished. My bedroom is quite simple, almost spartan: the bed where I lie, an angular walnut desk with spindly legs, a plain blue carpet on a hardwood floor, and walls papered in a pattern of tiny bouquets of violets alternating with an unidentifiable blue flower. I imagine the designer elected to dispense with notions of botany. Outside the door to the left there is a bathroom; to the right a hallway which passes her room and enters the living room, and adjoining that in another wing are the spacious dining room and kitchen. The facts are indeed simple. In order to pass from my bedroom to the kitchen I had to go through the whole house, which has a sizable collection of paintings. Moreover, I could not be expected to hear anything going on in the kitchen from my bedroom, whose door I keep closed and locked at all times, except when I use the adjoining bathroom which can only be reached via the hallway. Lastly the toilet never works properly even though we have spent a fortune in trying to have it fixed, replaced, and so forth; and during the period of time in question it was dripping and gargling loudly—loudly enough to mask any sounds in the farther reaches of the villa.

All these factors are crucial to the events that subsequently took place. I use the toilet frequently in the morning, not because of any bladder ailment, but rather for the slight amount of exercise it provides me—getting up from my bed, through the door, five steps down the hall, through the bathroom door, and back. And certainly it was during one of these little excursions that she slipped into my room, lifted the stack of magazines on the nightstand, and removed my notebook. I did not as a rule permit her in my room—which rule, however, was constantly being broken, either because I had to go out or because the door had no proper exterior lock, and so on. From these surreptitious visits she undoubtedly learned the whereabouts of the notebook. Being naturally trustful, I was careless of its hiding place. Easy enough to get at, I do confess. I should have been more careful.

But the weapon, a gun, is sure evidence of diabolical planning. A simple .22 pistol which I have traditionally stored in the desk drawer to defend myself against the possibility of nocturnal marauders. How she came to know of its whereabouts I do not know. Perhaps I mumbled something about it during one of our intimate sessions. But somehow she gained knowledge not only of it but also of the fact that I carry the key to the drawer in my right-hand trousers pocket. This is the white linen suit I put on after noon; before then I ramble around in a bright orange kimono-type bathrobe.

I imagine therefore that in the course of that crucial morning she entered my room no less than three times during the brief moments I was taking my morning constitutionals to the toilet. The first, to steal the notebook. The second, to lift the key from my trousers pocket. And the third, to unlock the drawer, remove the pistol and close and lock the drawer. Perhaps we can even suspect a fourth time, to return the key to my pocket in one of those irrational little gestures a criminal will make. Now we must suppose, the objects in her hands, a time lapse of, say, an hour during which she read the notebook cover to cover and resolved to commit the act she had so long been premeditating.

Yet while until now her movements had been masked by the neat conspiracy of natural events, her luck soon began to run out. She might have chosen to attack from the end of the hall as I was making another trip to the bathroom. She might have concealed herself in the bathroom and waited for me there, or in my room while I was out. All of these would have been virtually foolproof positions. Yet, for some incredible reason, she actually tried to force her way into my room while I was in it. As I said, I keep the door locked by way of a slide latch which is strong enough to delay though not block a forced entry. I was in bed when the door began to rattle and bulge. It was one of those moments when I feared the worst and knew my fears to be well-founded. Instinctively. Sooner or later. She has not been well, you know. Please note that I was in bed owing to the shock of having discovered my notebook missing—indeed stolen. I did not immediately suspect her of the theft because it seemed that there might be other people around more likely to have done it, but not to mention names. However, everything became clear in a flash as soon as the door started bulging and rattling. I knew it was her, that she had stolen the notebook, that she was coming to do a terrible thing, that I must escape immediately.

Jumping from bed, I ran to the window and threw it open and leaped to the soft lawn below. The villa is only one storey, the drop just a few feet. Then I ran across to some bushes where I concealed myself.

From that distance, ten or fifteen feet, I could still hear the door being pounded upon. I expected to hear it crash any minute. Yet suddenly the noise stopped and it was clear that she had not gained entry. This puzzled me, ultimately allayed my suspicions to the point that I re-entered the room via the window. Why had she failed to break the door down? There were all manner of heavy implements in the villa. Pokers, axes, shovels, and so on. Could it be that I was wrong? Perhaps she only wished to summon me for some important matter, such as a long-distance telephone call. I immediately dismissed all my suspicions, or most of them, and directed my attention back to the missing notebook. Still the question must be answered here and now: why did she fail to break into the room? I, not knowing the pistol was missing, would have said she suddenly realized that I might be standing behind the door with a loaded gun in my hand. But since in fact she did have it then, we can only assume that she was possessed by a murderous rage which rendered her, in some ways, physically impotent; she was capable of pulling triggers, but not of smashing down doors. In short, she was not being reasonable. We shall soon see how the application of this principle will ultimately explain all the facts of this case.

From then on the missing notebook occupied my mind to the exclusion of all other matters. I would have traded all my luggage for that one leather-bound notebook. Man is most vulnerable through his manuscripts. The irony being that only my closest of former friends can read my scratchy script, and of course there were none staying in the villa to my knowledge at that time. Thus, when I put on my white linen suit prior to setting off on my noon walk through the villa, my mind was so filled with the notebook that I had no inkling of what was awaiting me. Her strange behavior at the door had receded to a minor incident in the course of an eventful morning. But I failed to mention that some days before this moment the high-powered bulb in the ceiling fixture had blown out; and I had had quite enough of spending whole nights in my room in the dark and was thus resolved, that very morning, to take whatever steps were necessary to fetch a new bulb from the cupboard where they are stored in the kitchen. This also weighed on my mind. Also the burned-out bulb, which I had accidentally smashed, though I am not sure when, by flinging it against the wall.

I opened the door to the hall and stepped out. The villa was utterly quiet. The spacious hallway, hung with innumerable etchings, prints and photographs, was bathed in shadows too deep to encourage a casual investigation of its art. On soft and absent steps I advanced to the living room where I looked at the pictures a while. A very fine collection which the landlord of the villa has spent years assembling. I have been told that he is at work on a catalogue of his paintings so as to spare him the bother of explaining them to ignorant guests, which project I imagine he has suspended for the duration of his present world tour. In this fashionable resort, it seemed a supreme irony that a thief had broken into the villa and into my room to take my utterly worthless—in a negotiable sense—notebook while leaving thousands of dollars of paintings untouched on the walls. Or perhaps they are only reproductions. I am not an expert in these matters. I filled my pipe and made a few tours of the room. It is very comfortably furnished and I sat down now and then to rest. There was no hurry, I was taking my time. It takes me twenty minutes to smoke a bowlful, and when I had finished I carefully scraped the ashes into an ashtray on a marble-topped coffee table. These are now in the police laboratory for all to see.

Then I advanced through a sliding door to the spacious dining room, equally crowded with paintings. It was as quiet here as in the living room. Not a sound to be heard beyond the soft shuffle of my slippers around the room and a little hissing noise as I sucked on my pipe while contemplating the paintings. The sunlight pouring through the windows was especially pleasing. I was also keeping my eyes open for any signs of the notebook, or that slight displacement of an object which might indicate its presence nearby. But all was in order. The long dining table, its dozen or so chairs, its three slender unlit white candles. In the course of my slow perambulations, I generated an attractive layer of blue pipe smoke. Or was followed by one.

I was now at the kitchen door, which is of the swinging variety. Gently I pushed it, but there was some object on the floor inside the kitchen which was hindering its movement. I let the door fall back to its natural position, now inserted my fingernails in the crack and pulled it open towards me. It was my pistol, lying on the floor at the foot of the kitchen door. Now how are we to account for its seemingly inexplicable position? This will be answered in due course. The next thing that caught my attention was the oven door, which was wide open, and on the floor before it a box of matches with several expended ones scattered about. This modern gas range features a device which automatically turns off the entire gas supply in the event any one of the pilot lights goes off. Clearly she blew out the oven pilot light with the intention of putting on the gas and asphyxiating herself, but when this failed she attempted—again, irrationally—to relight the pilot, which is a very complicated operation that can be done only from the back of the range by professional servicemen. But this purposeless restoration of the order of things having failed, she became impatient. Were the pistol of a larger calibre, its distant position could be explained away by recoil, but since it was only a .22, we must assume that a last muscular spasm cast it across the room where it was stopped by the kitchen door. My notebook was on the kitchen table. I thought it wise to leave it there for the moment, there were other things to be done. I lifted the telephone receiver and dialed the police and, unfortunately, regrettably, my taste for melodrama made me utter an incredible line, something like: 'Something awesome has just happened to my wife!' What a day! They came fast. I stood there and awaited their arrival, not wishing to litter the pristine scene with gratuitous fingerprints.

The bullet-hole was like a tiny blue flower.

Which I cannot describe.

✦

Right off there was a misunderstanding. They wanted to know what I was doing there, would I please move aside while they did what they had to do. Most certainly I would. There were four of them, the one in charge had no uniform. An unseemly haste to get to the bottom of the mystery. They were obviously overworked and I feared they might botch the job, after all, a once-in-a-lifetime thing. What was one to do?

I paced around the villa a time in spite of my condition, then resolved to take the bull by the horns. The inspector was in the kitchen attempting to relight the pilot, the range had been pushed out from the wall, and one of the policemen was sweeping out the dust. At my reappearance, the inspector looked up and told me that tests had revealed that it had happened shortly before, indeed almost simultaneously with, my telephone call. This was an astounding piece of news. I hardly knew what to say. Why had I heard no *bang*? It immediately opened up another possibility which I had not foreseen even in my total bafflement before the facts—or so they seemed now—of the incident; that is, my first interpretation of suicide seemed much too hasty. She had not killed herself after all. But now I was faced with a problem of etiquette. Should I clear up this whole matter or let the police do it? For example, if I supplied too much information, they might become jealous of my powers of observation and detection and then slap an ungrounded charge on me. On the other hand, if I left everything up to them, they might make a grievous error. In the end I decided the risks of speaking out were less great. Silence condemns far more than even the most careless of words.

Therefore I announced in a loud and clear voice the theory of the masked intruder. The inspector dropped his wrench and stood up and transfixed me with an intense look. I resumed. Was not perhaps the possible murder the real clue to the crime? That was what I would try to answer. Now according to the theory of the masked intruder, shortly before I left my room *he* had entered the house by any one of the always unlocked doors, with the intention of stealing some of the extremely valuable (or valuable-looking) paintings, in an audacious broad-daylight art-theft such as one reads about in the newspapers. Naturally there is no reason for an outsider to suspect that the door adjoining the dining room leads to the kitchen; one could as well assume that it led to a sort of parlor where were kept, say, the most valuable of the paintings. And so the masked intruder, expert marksman that he was, stumbled through the kitchen door and discovered her with, of all things, a gun in her hand. Hail suburbia! He shot first and didn't miss. Now, of course, for the facts to fit the theory—and it was only a theory still—a number of things had to be established: the origin of the bullet, the number of cartridges left in the .22 pistol found at the foot of the kitchen door, traces of the masked intruder, or just one tiny trace, a seemingly unimportant detail. As for my not hearing the shot, if in fact it was fired while I was in the living room or dining room, his having used a silencer would account nicely for that.

The inspector appeared sufficiently interested that I invited him and his companions to stay for lunch, and it is to be recalled that one of the motives that drew me from my room in the first place was my traditional noontime hunger. I said it was no trouble—as soon as they got the range re-connected I could whip up something in a jiffy. After all, they would even be doing me a great service. He said they might stay, that they would have to see. I understood, he was on the job, couldn't formally say yes; so while they worked on the gas range I put out the makings for five of my special world-renowned bologna-like sandwiches (millions have been sold)—fortunately everything was in the refrigerator, a real bit of luck, since I had not anticipated this many for lunch, as usually there are no more than two of them—policemen—and now I carried everything out to the dining room and came back. A couple of them were standing around just watching the inspector fiddle with something in the range, so I told them to have no hesitation about looking through the notebook on the kitchen table, they could get a head-start. Which they did. They gave the binding a good going over, but thumbed through only a few pages, and hastily at that. They said it was very nice. I was famished and nibbled a bit on the sly. Also I carried out a number of bottles of fresh cold beer and soda pop.

At last they got the pilot relit and the range pushed back against the wall. I gave them fresh towels and soap and told them to use the kitchen sink, and when they were washed up I lured them into the dining room to the mouth-watering scene I had prepared. Concerning the masked intruder I had developed a few more ideas, in particular to account for the time problem, that is, those few seconds or minutes when we, he and I, might have been wandering simultaneously around the villa, and so forth. The inspector and his assistants were sufficiently interested in my ideas that they forgot themselves to the point of sitting down at the table. I told them to please eat. They did. Everything now seemed under control. I resumed. Now let us suppose that the masked intruder, perhaps an intimate of the landlord's villa, even a next-door neighbor, had been contemplating the theft for a long period of time, a number of years. Let us suppose furthermore that he was a veritable connoisseur of crime who wished to do everything not only with perfection but with a certain flair, with even that supreme audacity which is utterly spellbinding to those exposed to it. After all, by definition, thieves of art treasures must be aesthetes, and it is not a long step from there to say that they must be actors, that they are sublime actors. Let us suppose finally that the masked intruder, from his next-door vantage point, has been waiting many years for the opportunity that will fit his considerable talents, which cannot be exercised in the presence of the landlord, who knows him just a bit too well. But!—the landlord suddenly takes a world tour, rents his villa out to us. All the time thinking that it will be in the excellent care of his friend the next-door neighbor, who will keep an eye out. However, please note that my accusations at this point are strictly hypothetical, based on well-founded hearsay. As for the proof, that will come later, the proof that the masked intruder is the next-door neighbor.

But perhaps we ought to pause now to consider the person of this masked intruder. What does he look like? How tall is he? Weight? Apparent facial structure? They seemed interested in these questions, though with mouths filled with my tasty food they were in no condition to do anything but nod. However, I went on, here lies a danger, for if we are to imagine him as definite of feature now in a bit-by-bit reconstruction, we will take away some of his charm; if we make of him a solid, three-dimensional human being at this very early stage of the investigation, we shall probably find him much too bulky, much too slow of movement to complete the difficult task which, if we are to believe our eyes, he has already carried out. Far better that he retain all his purity for the moment. And if he is the true actor we suppose he is, what does it really matter what he looks like?

Now perhaps you begin to see. Frequently in the afternoon I take strolls through the villa's spacious gardens, and from any number of places I can be observed from the outlying villas. Indeed, with high-powered binoculars, my every gesture and facial movement and detail of dress will become almost microscopically visible. Little will I realize that I am being minutely observed from another rooftop or through the hedges as I bend over to sniff the roses, as I pluck a snail from a begonia pot, as I watch the goldfish in the pond and drop them scraps of bread; and how can I ever guess that the details of my person are being lifted one by one to be reassembled next door as part of a subtle disguise? I can't. So I am literally stolen. You see now the masked intruder practicing being myself by night before tripartite mirrors, you see him mastering the trick, you may even see him venturing out to dare my usual haunts with a phantom shadow of myself, perhaps even—in a most audacious test—standing one night facing my fireplace with his back to the living room, grunting in agreement to one of her probably inane remarks, until she leaves the room and he presently vanishes into the void from which he has come—while all this time I am resting up in my room, without the slightest inkling that my very existence is being woven into a fantastical plot.

I told them to help themselves to some beer or, if they couldn't drink on the job, some soda pop. Now I cautioned them here against assuming the masked intruder was a novice at this sort of thing. Most certainly not. To carry off an audacious art-theft such as he contemplated without prior experience or practice would be unthinkable. Now it was a matter of fact that the landlord, a strange fellow from what I could see of him by way of his valuable villa, possessed in his garage a completely dismantled brand-new automobile. Would they like to see it? The inspector and his assistants nodded this way and that, neither clearly yes nor no. Well it wasn't really necessary to see it now. They were still hungry, wanted to eat. Now this automobile, taken completely to pieces by the landlord, lay in curious little heaps of metal all over the floor of the garage. A pretty sight in a way, I added. According to the neighbors, the landlord and his next-door neighbor—the masked intruder—had been the closest of friends for many years, best friends even, at least to all outward appearances. Differences will arise, and unseen. We can imagine the masked intruder watching the landlord take apart this automobile, watching with the greatest fascination. And thinking.

Why the landlord wanted to possess a completely dismantled automobile, I do not know, but that is what he wanted and that was what he thought he had. Then something began to happen. The automobile started reassembling itself, very small parts not readily distinguishable to the casual observer started combining in an indescribable manner. In the gloom of the garage, it is generally believed that the landlord noticed none of this. But I, upon moving into the villa, did. And I conclude that it was the masked intruder who undertook these little rearrangements in secret. Why? Now I said before that the art-theft was a supremely audacious act carried out under my watchful eye. Such skill must have been acquired, it was the skill of surreptitiously rearranging small details, one by one, in such a way as to deceive even those who thought they were observing carefully, who saw nothing, felt nothing, until the very moment the carpet under their feet was gone, until the vertigo of utterly thin air. Thus, in order for the masked intruder to carry out the theft of bulky objects in plain daylight, he needed to perfect his methods by way of practice, and where he first practiced was in the gloom of the garage, upon a collection of metal objects which the landlord thought he knew intimately. We can see now the masked intruder slipping into the garage, perhaps every morning at a fixed hour, to rearrange and refit some part, but only slightly, ever so slightly, in such a way that the landlord, upon examining his collection of metal each morning, would never notice any one thing amiss, though he might well walk away with a slight sense of malaise which he would ascribe to another cause. And had he not gone off on his travels so suddenly, the masked intruder might have kept on with his subtle manipulations to create, say, a metallic monster of a sort never seen before, never seen before up to the final moment of completion, the tightening of the last bolt—when the landlord would at last open his eyes and see with an awful shock that his automobile had *grown* into something beyond describing.

But since the landlord went away, that project came to an abrupt end, and the masked intruder immediately set in motion the preliminary phases of his art-theft. And perhaps here we ought to ask why the masked intruder stepped across that line which separates a private garage prank from a public crime, a crime which may well lead to a prison term of no mean length, and other unpleasant consequences. The reason we are all sitting together at this table. What brought us together. I asked my companions whether they had enough to eat—there were still more sandwiches on the plate. They had to be eaten up, you know. They protested. But I passed around the plate and in the end they accepted another serving, and the dining room was once again filled with pleasant smacking sounds. Now it was clear, I went on, that the masked intruder was a man who delighted in intricate deception. Some might say that he got carried away into committing a public crime. But I thought rather that he had done it deliberately. After all, there was little art—or rather interest—in deceiving or stealing from one man, whereas it required the greatest skill to steal from many or all. Thus, in committing a deliberate public crime, though ostensibly directed against his best friend the landlord, the masked intruder was placing himself in the unique position of having to survive by his skill alone from now on, for the police and everyone else would soon be against him. He would know, the moment he made a careless move, that he would be caught, and his being caught would be the proof that he was losing his touch, agonizing proof, in the peculiar all or nothing of the art-theft trade. And this, I ventured, was precisely what he wanted. He wanted the all or nothing. He wanted to be balanced upon that *or*, upon that tight-wire, and the balancing was the all, and beneath was the nothing, black or white—no grey, no grey at all. To steal paintings? The choice of the crime was almost insignificant. Except in so far as it led to the proof of the identity of the masked intruder, as in order for him to steal *anything* he must virtually abandon *everything* he owned, he could not sit around in one spot, he had to move, constantly move on. A painting?—something he could embrace only at the instant of theft, to be followed by a perpetual separation. He might always envy his victims' sense of possession, a feeling he could never afford, he would only feel constant loss, constant loss as he moved on, circulated, wandered, only touching things, never holding them, across the many continents of this world. He must travel. And that is why I said the masked intruder was the next-door neighbor. Whom I have never met, let alone seen. But he is off traveling somewhere—and now, undoubtedly, in a distant land selling off the landlord's paintings to finance another and more daring theft.

It remains for us to reconstruct the definitive day of the crime, now that we have established both his identity and motives. The masked intruder, having first stolen and mastered myself through watching me afternoons in the garden, begins to wonder what I am up to all morning long, since I do not make my appearance outside until some time after two. There is a tense day as he flits in and out of the villa, from closet to unused room, to locate the position and nature of my morning presence. He is in luck. He discovers that I remain in my room, with brief and unproblematic exceptions, until exactly noon. He will turn my own punctuality to his own uses—and against me. He assumes that she is equally punctual. But there he is wrong. She is not punctual. It is interesting to note that, like so many, the masked intruder miscalculates women. Yet we cannot determine at this point whether he has made a mistake or not. I think so, but my opinions must be taken for their objective worth. But it is now time to put the final touches on the master plan. Perhaps he patiently grows a bushy red beard. Or shaves one off. Hell with that! An unimportant detail! Item: the mask. He has observed from my afternoon walks and perhaps from a chance encounter that I am something of a prankster, correctly deduces that she will see nothing exceptional in my walking around the villa with a mask on; indeed, this detail will not so much cover up his identity as convince her beyond all doubts that this masked man is myself, and she will see, or not see, because of his mastery, a white linen suit, my unsteady gait, my manner of holding my hands— she will see *myself,* she will see my spitting image, as it were, while all this time he, the masked intruder, will not *be* me, for if he really is, his whole plan will collapse or be unthinkable: what invalid can endure this performance? So he simply feigns this aspect of my person. My slow but graceful walk, my habit of sitting down to rest every few steps, and so on. I am an invalid by purely philosophical decision, mind you, the decision to do nothing at all, for what is there to do? And movement, especially rapid movement, is the drug of the time, as may be witnessed from the dashing character of the masked intruder himself. Thus, if she chances to stumble upon him, masked of face and somewhat creaky of gesture, while he is removing the paintings from the walls, she will see nothing unusual in it, find nothing extraordinary in his not saying a word, for certainly in his prowlings around he has discovered that we are not on speaking terms at the moment. And even if she sees him shuffling out the front door under a load of paintings, she will not give this more than a brief second thought, for on occasion, rare it may be, I do summon together my strengths to venture forth to see what is going on out there, in the so-called outside world. As usual, nothing.

But the masked intruder is faced with one last problem. The paintings will be missed. There will be investigations. The theft will be discovered. Now as you know, there are both simple crimes and mixed crimes, and it is much more difficult to solve the latter.

The masked intruder chose then to commit a mixed crime so as to confuse the nature and motives of the theft, and he chose murder. And here we must assume that he gained possession of my .22 pistol—but how? Who knows? So at last we lose the thread of this genius's movements. That he acquired the pistol is beyond doubt, but his means must forever be concealed—short of a confession—from our earthly eyes. The imagination boggles at the dance-like movements our actor-masked-intruder has to go through to obtain the weapon from my desk drawer, the key from my trousers pocket, and so on, all without arousing my suspicions or hers, and, we must assume, the very same morning as the crime.

But, you will ask, looking up from your tasty bologna-like sandwiches, the walls show no signs of missing any paintings. At first glance that seems to be the case, which I do not deny, even before a thorough-going investigation has been carried out. But let us first return to the masked intruder's master plan. His intention is to steal the paintings from around eleven thirty in the morning till noon. The simple crime thus committed successfully, he then transforms it into a mixed crime by murdering her in the kitchen at, say, five minutes to noon, just at the time I am preparing to abandon my room for my daily stroll through the villa. This schedule is extremely important. He shoots her, vanishes, and then I innocently walk on to the scene of the mixed crime, perhaps stoop over to pick up the weapon lying in the way of the kitchen door—and immediately convict myself of murder! What a stroke of genius! Or, even supposing I do not pick up the gun or suddenly realize what I have done and wipe off the fingerprints, yet there I am at the scene of the crime virtually within five minutes of its having been committed, with no other suspects in sight. A few days later, of course, someone gets around to discovering that a few paintings are missing, and for no extra charge and in the interest of tidiness I am accused of having salted them away somewhere—which I deny as vehemently as the murder itself. But who will believe me?

So much for the master plan. Now for its execution. Clearly he failed. From what we can see there are no paintings missing. What went wrong? If I remember correctly I left my room somewhat earlier than usual. He probably heard my footsteps approaching down the hall. Why didn't he simply slip away from the villa, to come back another day? No, impossible. For our masked intruder, a man of supreme discipline, has put all his stakes on this one day. Imagine a getaway car, an expensive plane ticket, hotel reservations in distant cities, and so on. Thus, at the sound of my footsteps he is seized by the realization that his master plan is, at this chosen moment, entirely unworkable. At least here, in the villa. But he can still salvage part of it. So he slips away from the villa, climbs in his getaway car and goes off traveling somewhere, vanishing without perhaps leaving a trace. Which remained to be seen. A very remarkable man, I thought.

The policemen were utterly spellbound by my explanation. I told them, please feel free to use the telephone to send out a search party for the masked intruder, if they wished; also, if they would like to move into the living room, I would bring them some coffee. They were agreeable to the last suggestion, and I went into the kitchen and poured out five cups from the pot I had put on to heat. I rejoined them in the living room. They were standing around at odd angles, hands in their pockets, looking at the paintings. A truly impressive collection of contemporary art, as the landlord calls it, though contemporary to whom? Not me, surely. Art is timeless, the epoch of no importance. I expressed a certain satisfaction at finding none apparently missing, which seemed to please them no end. We sipped coffee. At last the inspector ventured to ask me what a number of the paintings meant, what did they represent, why were they represented that way. I could see he was a simple though well-meaning man. A pleasantry was most definitely called for. Well, I said, as soon as they caught the masked intruder, then they would find out. He was surely an expert, would be delighted to talk about them at great length—indeed, he would have little else to do. They all laughed.

Only one could I tell them anything about in fact, and for that I beckoned them to stand at a certain spot in the dining room, facing what seemed to be a picture window—as it actually was. Yet from that spot the woman of the purple range was so perfectly framed that she appeared to be a painting inside the very room, hanging from the wall. They murmured the deepest of appreciations: explained that the landlord had constructed his entire villa around this view at the greatest expense, and as they could see the effect was overwhelming, and they did agree that it was the finest eye-sleight they had ever seen.

After coffee they decided to get down to the serious business of searching the villa, large though it may be, of innumerable wings. Of course they could use the landlord's vacuum cleaner. Why not? So with it they went over the kitchen, dining room, living room, hallway, and so on. I showed them the bathroom. The whistling toilet. My private bedroom. Here they expressed great interest in my expensive tape-recording system which takes up half one wall of my bedroom, and gladly I set about entertaining them with the latest results of my travels. They made themselves comfortable on my bed. I played. First, pleasantly intermingled with my narrative, came the very mellow tones of the dirigible's calliope as it went through its repertory of sentimental tunes prior to taking off, which was part of the helium pump. As I recall, this is the world's largest flying organ, though sadly my machine was not up to recording the vast range of tones, or, rather, many were probably marred by the toilet and other house noises. They didn't seem to mind. Now came the cacophonous dance of the savages which, as you recall, was performed on a sheet-metal platform held up by a bamboo frame, producing an incredible thundering and clattering effect until the platform collapsed on to the bonfire underneath it with the sound of a high roar of wind—and many shrieks. Also the sound of me patting out what I feared was a fire in my hair. Admittedly that bit of tape was not too coherent. Then the morning song, addressed to the rising sun (I have been told), of a mountain hermit to the accompaniment of his hand-made folk lyre, a very charming ditty which I cannot praise too highly, though some will complain of its length. The strings of the lyre are made of the finest of gut, hence the delicate tones. I explained to the policemen that that was all I had on this tape, a fresh one which I began only a week ago, and that I had recorded the hermit's song only a day before I got here, while crossing some mountains. If they wished I could put on my other tapes. No, they said, standing up from the bed, but the inspector did want to know how I obtained my richness of tone (I protested!) which seemed to emanate from the very depths of the villa. I explained that the machine was connected to speakers in every room of the house and to others sitting in trees in the garden, in such a way that there was virtually no soundproof corner, which enhanced not only the tones but the general effect. They could not but agree, saying however that they had better be moving on to the next case. It was a hard life, I knew, and much did I appreciate their quick response to my call. I escorted them to the door of my room, where I thanked them again and paid the usual fee. They said they could find their own way out of the villa.

✦

However they left me with a person lurking about the villa. So I locked myself securely in my room until such time as I might recover the strength to find and expel the person, as the recent flurry of activity had rendered me needful of a substantial rest. Sleep, no. Sleep was not easy with the entire villa at the disposition of the person outside that door and no idea of what the person might do; I lay uneasily in bed all that night, microphone in hand, occasionally broadcasting through the villa's convenient public address system polite requests that the person leave at once and be so kind as to signal the person's departure by ringing the doorbell three times, which I could confirm by peeking out my bedroom window and thus avoid falling into a trap, such as being forced into eating an abominable apple pie.

But the person did not leave, or if the person left, made no noise about it, and my spirit of rest would be shattered beyond repair until I really knew and, if necessary, forced an eviction once and for all; and tired as I was, the next morning towards noon I went and shaved and put back on my white linen suit, to venture forth once again into the rest of the villa. Though, as a precaution to mask my footsteps, I first put on a speeding express train tape which is realistic beyond believing. The villa then thundered and hooted from all corners, and little do I care what the neighbors think since I do not live here and, I am sure, they know it; why we are on such good terms. The hallway was completely deserted except for a trembling of the glass covering the innumerable prints and photographs lining the long walls. Although the bedroom next to mine, which belonged to the landlord's wife, was locked, the landlord had provided me with a set of keys for emergencies such as this and I now put them to use. The room appeared to be empty. I looked around. In the wardrobe packed and hung with her expensive clothing, in a dressing table littered with empty bottles of perfume and cologne and bits of oddly shaped metal and plastic, under the bed, in a case packed with old letters, nowhere was the person to be found. I locked up the room.

The hallways were still deserted. I crept to the living room which, because of its impressive collection of bulky furniture, was a tricky place to search and no telling how the person might pop out from behind an over-stuffed chair or drop from the very chimney, already spinning devices against my unwittingly turned back. But I took this chance, and searched. Nothing was there under the sofa and various chairs and in a variety of cabinets filled only, as it turned out, with the landlord's junk, and elsewhere, everywhere. I stepped into the dining room, looked around, and decided not to bother with the enormous china cupboard, where anyone's breathing would have sent up a tinkling audible even over the roar of the interminable express train. Yet something seemed wrong in that room. I advanced a half-pace. And then saw. On the east wall the frame still hung, but through or inside it was nothing but a quiet, hazy suburban scene—the woman of the purple range was gone! Utterly gone! So the masked intruder had finally struck. I was dumbfounded. A most extraordinary coup! I sat down and stared through the now empty glass. Trees, a distant house, a segment of winding road, a most ordinary landscape. How could I ever explain my lapsed vigilance to the poor landlord? His most valuable painting, around which he had constructed the entire villa—now gone. His villa practically worthless. How could I ever indemnify the poor man? What could I do?

✦

I sat for some time at the dining room table, its three thin white candles smeared yellow by an unaccustomed light flooding through the picture window, and thought about many things. But that would not help. And I felt like moving. So I wandered on, into the second long hallway which is off the dining room and which cuts short, right, into the kitchen wing of the villa, while another branch extends straight to a bath and two more bedrooms. Towards these two I now went; originally intended by the landlord to house his children and eventual heirs, they were now locked up and had never been used owing to the fact that he and his charming young wife, for all their real estate, were childless, and the rooms, as I unlocked them one after the other, were as bare as could be imagined, devoid of either carpet, furniture, or pictures on the wall; and thus I locked them up. Nor was there anyone in the bathroom, other than someone noisily taking a shower. To be ignored. The villa had been rented that way.

By now a full day had passed since I had last opened up my diet of fresh air to indulge in solid food, and I was hungry, trembling a little in the knees even, as I retraced my steps and swung into the villa's spotless modern kitchen, where I knew there would be food to eat. Thus, pushed on by my traditional noontime hunger, I searched out food and constructed one of my world-famous bologna-like sandwiches, my sole daily food, and set about the eating of it. Yet it was not as tasty as some I have made, it tasted definitely inferior; and looking up from the sandwich, perhaps stale, in this kitchen blocked out by the many light-hued forms of the latest and largest appliances the landlord's money could buy for his wife, once a year like automobiles, looking up from the smears of my plate, I was overcome by the distinct sensation that something was beginning to go wrong. Which should be stopped.

Thus, upon wolfing down the sandwich, I proceeded straight to a nap on a small couch I have had especially installed in the kitchen, rather than return all the way through the dining room, living room and the long hall for the very same nap to be had, as it were, in my own bedroom, but at the expense of a tiring walk. I slept, but not well, and awoke to a fatigue greater than that which had thrown me down, as one will awake to a sense of not having got anywhere at all, in the same room, the same house, which has been intractable against the effects of time, has refused to change; and that is why I decided to call it a day and go back to my room.

Early next morning, in a change of tactics, I rose and dressed and carried out a cursory inspection of the villa, in a new silence almost total, so as to have an early start on the garden, which has been neglected of late. Constructed along the best of imported traditions which dictate that the plants nearest the house be the most groomed and cultivated, the garden begins, properly speaking, as a sort of courtyard half-enclosed by the kitchen and unused-bedroom wings of the villa, and from there extends with progressive wildness several acres yonder to the bosky horizon of a tangle of untrimmed vegetation. And so an examination would be best conducted upon the same principle, though inverted: hasty in the carefully cultivated areas, careful in the distant areas of hasty, untrained growth. Advancing then across the shaded courtyard of potted tropical plants, I interwove an inspecting path amongst the landlord's statuary, a fine collection of pleasingly mounted contemporary debris, rusting and corroding with the greatest abandon, until the lawn and its stone pathways ended in clumps of low-lying bushes penetrated by narrow gravel-surfaced ambles, sinuous of arabesque, which radiated from a central fish pond of no mean dimensions. And where I rested a moment on a stone bench. The sun was indeed hot that morning, its light penetrated into the very depths of the greenish waters of the pond to spot in flames some dozen fat goldfish, who were swimming in atavistic course (for the pond was too large) towards becoming nothing more than carp. In a few years they would have to be changed.

I went on. The gravel ambles led to a haphazard network of simple dirt tracks through thickets of flowering shrubbery the height of a man and interspersed with open circular spaces where grew fruit trees of all varieties compatible with the climate, which was generous; and beyond, simple leaf trees which bore no fruit and sprang high from clumps of brush and fern and patches bare of all but matted leaves; until the garden was no longer a garden, but a thick forest, whose uncertain lease on the earth was marked only by a dribbling sprinkler-head deep in the shadows, which would erupt in spray automatically towards nightfall along with scores of others. I pushed through twig and low-hanging bough, stepping over the points of a dropped branch, through the densest part of the forest, to break through into a narrow band completely clear but for a low cover of dry grasses, a fence, a narrow asphalt road, beyond which lay the solid green wall of a neighbor's fruit grove.

And standing on the other side of the fence, exactly opposite the point where I broke through, facing me, indeed seeming to stare at me with a special intensity, perhaps out of wondering what had been crashing through the forest at that point, was a man, arms folded, legs apart and cigarette burning. A man such as gives one pause. Something was acutely out of shape with his whole form, clothed in an expensive tan suit; towering he was, over six feet, but too wide, much too wide, and oddly flat. Perhaps he was built that way. The suit fitted tightly in places, slackly in others. I noticed these things first while trying to examine the head, which could not be taken in at one glance. So extraordinary was it. Topped by long, flowing red hair, combed straight back, with the suggestion of a part in the middle. There were dark glasses, rimmed in heavy black plastic. A nose of record length descended from bushy eyebrows, chestnut-like of color, to cleave a rich mustache which flowed in gentle curve to suggest both hairy wings and a sort of fixed smile, perhaps benign, perhaps knowing. The mustache practically concealed the entire mouth, letting pass only the dull gleam of yellow teeth clenched upon a cigarette generating a merciful fog before his entire visage.

He stood immobile, stiffly immobile. As if a gesture, as if even a slight movement might snowball into a menacing blow such as would fell a fence post, wreak havoc, spread fear. Thus I walked up to him with the utmost caution and though not introducing myself explicitly made it clear that I belonged here and knew what I was doing. Only the fence now separated us. I could hear his breathing.

But he remained otherwise silent. His cigarette burned slowly down to the filter, then dropped from his teeth to the ground. He made not one move. I squinted and peered through his very dark glasses. His eyes were closed. Good afternoon, I said softly. But he was asleep—sleeping on his feet.

I withdrew a few paces, wondering what to do. I felt obliged to wake the man, for sleeping on foot at the side of a public road was not the wisest or safest thing to do, but could not think how

I might. Not with a loud noise, which is unpleasant. And the man had a monstrous air about him. A well-chosen word, shouted or sung, would be far better. But what word? The situation hardly called for the use of the word 'love'. Which might cause some terrible misunderstanding. But something warm to wake up by, yet non-committal. Finally, after much thought I hit upon a word and placed myself squarely before him, just out of reach of his long arms, fixed a radiant smile on my face, spread my palms, and with the full force of my lungs shouted 'SUNSHINE!'

He opened his eyes and blinked.

```
This be a recording. What?
```

he or something replied in a thick but weak voice. From, perhaps, the depths of his coat. Though his mouth, behind the mustache, might have moved. He stepped sideways, heavily, towards a fence post, upon which he dropped a weighty elbow to lean. I heard something crack. He tipped his enormous head down and stared at me over the top of his dark glasses.

```
What?
```

Nothing, I replied, nothing at all, except that I was just wondering who he might be and whether in need of assistance.

```
I be the Plainclothman, with capital
letter. Take note please. I Plainclothman
survey this property with eye multi-
professional. It declines going anywheres.
As such, arrested. With the single hand.
Applause, please. Thank you, oh thank you
very much. Very kind. Now we can have a
joint walk to demonstrate my many foreign
accents. One hobby of mine. Fascinates.
With a mouth large of birth. We shall now
walk.
```

I had no time to object. He swung a huge foot into the air and brought it down on top of the rusting wire fence, which sagged, and I stepped across to his side and jumped a culvert to the pavement. Muttering away in his peculiar garbled voice he joined me with the clattering leap of a great bird which could never quite fly, and we set off down the road at an uncomfortably rapid pace. He was a strange walker, loosely fitted, as if his body contained an extra supplement of vertebrae, musculature or misplaced fat tissue; he was seemingly uncoordinated, bouncy, like a man with parcels stuffed inside his coat. Somewhere he squeaked. I first thought it was in the shoes, but no, it was higher up, somewhere in the legs, a regular, rasping squeak. For all his great size, almost toppling bulk, his ferocious expression—quite monster-like—there was something that seemed to render him harmless and ineffectual, perhaps in his weak, distant voice, twisted by indescribable accents. After a time, fearing this might be the beginnings of an onrush of curiosity-seekers, I asked him exactly what his connection with the case was, if any, beyond what he had said.

> None. Closed. Shut up. I be, incidentally, the new man. Applause please. Thank you, yes thank you very much. A handsome attendance this morning, good for the heart. Now, the case. Closed for lack of facts. I be the man of facts. Thank you. The facts be and must be got straight, each one in its little box with no strings attaching. Each fact contains a thing, certainly nothing wrong with that, and neatly displayed, arranged in rows, there be no connection. Can't be. Case, I said, closed. You better know, in fact, you better know. Now! I be. I be in fact in entirety the world-famed, no less than, the Grand Detective, with capital lettering. You better know that. Thank you, thank you ever so much. Please, no more applause.

I sighed, wondering what this creature was trying to tell me, and made an ambiguous gesture, perhaps of throwing up my hands.

> Do not touch! Stay! Hold! No one shakes the hand of the Grand Detective. His—my—fingerprints not to be had so easily as that. No tricks! Furthermore I be the performing amateur ventriloquist, without capital letters. Theref—

There what?

>  Theref—Hell! Conse—Theref—

Therefore?

>  —ore I can, may even, I be expert at designing confession, putting words into mouths any chosen moment. Any. Just like that! Though by preference I do imitations of natural force and powerful things. Nothing small or petty. The elements. The thunderstorms. The earthquakes. The raging seas. The volcanic eruptings. Floods. Locomotives. Bombings. And charmingly done large animals. To now demonstrate. Shh! Listen!

I listened. He puckered up his mouth and made the sound of running water.

>  The giraffe!

What?

>  Peeing.

Well. I thought it best to compliment him on his performance and said it was exceedingly well done.

>  Such be my powers. Indeed, universal be they. Thank you, thank you. Requests for more, please. May I recommend the world-renowned alligator sneeze? Aah—

No, thank you, I interrupted, I really had to be getting back. At his fast pace we had already walked some distance down the road and were now at the edge of a sort of forest preserve. I stopped and made as if to part ways and retrace my steps, for I could not see how I might benefit further from this man's performances. Charming they might be, but I was in no mood. And if the truth be known, I was convinced of a probable madness. There could be no other way to account for his increasingly obvious disguise, but of course that was no help. To know it was a disguise. A man disguised is neither more nor less than that. It was an odd neighborhood.

Well, glad to have met you, I said, offering my hand.

    Never!

he cried in a high-pitched voice, recoiling a few steps. Then, suddenly, to the sound of something ripping inside his clothes—or should I say, upholstery?—he made a lunge. I stumbled to one side. He missed. The next thing I knew I was plowing through some bushes, pursued by his thunderous footsteps and ever-quickening squeak, heaving pantings and a booming

    I be the Grand Detective! One! Two! One! Two!

I broke through the bushes into a thick forest of fir-like trees and dodged between the trunks in a zigzag course. I feared he might have a gun. His squeak suddenly turned into a harsh rasping noise, displeasing to the ear. It sounded like he was gaining. Yet the trees made up an attractive forest, which I might have chosen to admire at greater length under more favorable circumstances, and I was no little annoyed to have to pass up, with a quick jump, a fetching little stream clogged with plant- and wildlife. But at the least, during the briefest of instants, I was able to forget that I was being pursued by some tiresome neighbor. In the glitter of a quick scan of the eye. Such are the consolations of nature. Then from behind me came a terrible crash, and silence.

I stopped running and looked back. He had apparently vanished. Retracing my steps among the trees, which were growing quite thickly in here, I came to a spot which resembled the scene of an airplane crash. He had hit a tree and had literally come apart. To one side of the trunk lay his dark glasses, broken in two pieces, his mop of red hair, which was a wig, bits of hair—the remains of his mustache and bushy eyebrows. A large rubber nose. False teeth made out of wax. A shoe had come off—an elevator shoe. His coat was split in two places, revealing stuffings made out of wadded-up pages covered all over with an indecipherable script.

Gently I rolled him—or it—over on his back.

> Help me out of this thing!

he groaned. I saw now that he was a rather small man inside the thing he was wearing, a thing somewhat like a musical instrument case in the form of a man, hinged at the joints and covered with paper padding underneath the tan suit. With his right hand he indicated stiffly a number of metal clasps inside his coat and down one side of the case. I unlatched these and tried to pry the case open.

> Pull! Harder!

At last, by ripping the suit all the way down to his ankles, I was able to fling the lid back. There he lay, a small man, dressed in bright orange pyjamas. He raised his hand, I pulled him to his feet, and he limped around in circles, swearing softly, massaging bruises and scratches. He still wore one large rubber ear. The other eyed us from the tree trunk upon which it had become stuck. After a time he bent over the case in the form of a man, tore off the rest of the suit and stuffed it inside, along with the other bits and pieces and paper padding, closed the lid, sat on it and fastened the clasps. But when he tried to lift it, he almost fell over. I offered to carry it for him.

He stared at me intently, then made a gesture of assent. I hoisted the thing up on my shoulders—it was indeed heavy—and we went on our way, such as it was. I could no longer say. But his barefooted limp made for slow going and seemed to get worse, for by the time we had broken through to another road which promised to lead us back from whence we had come, he was tiptoeing along in a most cringing manner, hissing at the pain. And the pavement, hot under the noon sun and spotted with sharp gravel, appeared to be even more unbearable. He was a curious fellow, short, with light sandy hair and green eyes, a face marked with chronic ill-humor. For which he had good enough cause now, though I could not think how to obtain an explanation for his recent spectacular behavior. He did not seem interested in my presence anymore and greeted a cheerful remark on the fine quality of the weather with a leaden silence.

By an accident of circularity, we were now approaching the front of the villa, but at a pace that must have seemed motionless to the fast-walking passerby. The man's knees were becoming wobbly. I asked him whether he was all right. But he ignored me again. His eyes went half-closed, his teeth clenched, he began bobbing up and down, weaving this way and that. I took him by the arm to straighten his course, and in case he might suddenly drop. Now close, I could hear him talking. Chattering away. Almost inaudibly.

```
I told them. I told them it would never
work. Never. Do anything? Be anything?
I told them. They knew it all along. I
quit. Finished. Find someone else. What
do they want? But not me. Going back
to her white thighs. Pendant breasts.
Vacation. A little trip. Trees. Birds.
Air. Air. I—
```

but he choked, and started coughing.

I guided him up the path to the front door of the villa, through a handsome collection of shrubbery and, one by one, up the front steps. I was now supporting most of his weight on one arm. Easing the case in the form of a man to the ground, I leaned over and rang the doorbell with my free hand. After a moment the shadow of a woman glided across a picture window and the door opened.

She took the both of us in at a glance and immediately thanked me for bringing her husband home. It would seem the situation was not new to her. She said she could manage, slipping her arm around his waist while I detached his fingers from their strong grip on my coat sleeve. They closed on her right breast. His eyes were shut and he was breathing heavily. She inched him across the threshold, slowly, gently, and with a backward toss of the head asked me if I could be so kind as to carry the case just inside the door. Of course. She thanked me again. I said goodbye and closed the door softly behind me.

I stood on the front steps a moment, gazing down this quiet residential street, which stretched interminably into the distance. Then, although somewhat tired myself, I regained the sidewalk to resume the way which was mine.

✦

I have purchased a new notebook.

Which now I must describe.

By actual count it contains many pages; these are unlined, unnumbered, edges dipped in gilt, and can be turned one by one, forwards or backwards, by means of a spring mechanism actuated by a button on the binding. Covered with the finest of green leathers and featuring an internal heater for cold-weather operation, the notebook contains an ample spine in which can be found an extendable writing lamp, small but powerful, a pen and pencil holder, an ink bottle, erasers and a ruler. A special device enables the user to lock the notebook closed in such a way that it cannot be opened without involving complete destruction of the pages, and in this position also a special handle enables one to use the notebook as an effective weapon, something like a mace; or the user can lock the notebook open flat, in which position four telescopic legs of a patented design can be extended from the covers to the ground in such a way that the notebook can serve as a small writing desk; and inside the hollow legs are lightweight tubular fittings which can be assembled in thirty seconds flat to form a sturdy chair, or can be used as tentpoles, or by way of an optional wiring system can function as an antenna for the miniature shortwave radio, also in the binding. However, either of the latter two usages precludes attaching a separate adaptor package, no larger than a handsome volume of reproductions, which consists of two lightweight wheels, a number of cables, joints and swivels; these, when attached in the standard time of two minutes, convert the notebook into a small bicycle which can be ridden very fast indeed over the roughest of terrain.

*Kuala Lumpur—Rangoon—Madras—*
*Samarkand—Aleppo—Benghazi—*
*Constantine—Brasilia—Tumaco—*
*San Francisco—Fairbanks—Kyoto*

*January, 1967*